BEES & DISEASE
(THE BUCK WEEDLEMAN INTERVIEWS)

BEES & DISEASE
(THE BUCK WEEDLEMAN INTERVIEWS)

Volume 7—Black Friday

WILLIAM RUSSELL JACOBS &
CHRISTOPHER A. STOOPS

iUniverse, Inc.
Bloomington

Bees & Disease (The Buck Weedleman Interviews)
Volume 7 - Black Friday

iUniverse books may be ordered through booksellers or by contacting:

iUniverse
1663 Liberty Drive
Bloomington, IN 47403
www.iuniverse.com
1-800-Authors (1-800-288-4677)

ISBN: 978-1-4620-4651-5 (sc)
ISBN: 978-1-4620-4652-2 (ebk)

Printed in the United States of America

iUniverse rev. date: 08/10/2011

Once upon a time . . .

The reclusive, elusive, enigmatic and inspired Buck Weedleman visited a pearl of a city, adjacent to a free port on the Pecatonica River, and surprised three researchers having a drink at the Yellow Creek Inn. Our trip begins there. Weedleman, while considered delusional by some, is perhaps strangely enlightened in his lost reality like a hero in a fairytale blissfully unaware that he exists within the fairytale. I don't know. I can only report what he said in response to a few questions I posed. I found Weedleman's demeanor to be kind yet caustic, authentic yet obstinate, genuine yet hidden from perception, heroic yet villainous, or perhaps just captivating. Buck Weedleman's reality is either that of a true visionary or a deluded parody; Reality or delusion—I guess that's for you to decide.

Much has already been written about the travels and philosophy of Buck Weedleman. He is an icon. He is a legend. I found him to be a semi-optimistic iconoclast. Science has long claimed that he possesses the evolutionary capabilities that the rest of humanity will not possess for at least the next 4 to 5 hundred years. Religions are split as to the root causes of Buck's existence—some claim Weedleman's existence as an act of divine intervention, while others simply accept Weedleman as divine.

A version of this book was planned for release during the 2010 Christmas season strictly incorporating several years of research and study of Weedleman. We, as authors and empirically based scientists, maintained silence as to the topic of our biography/ study and analysis so as to not create upheaval within and among the scientific communities, religious sects, and populous variants independent of science and religion.

However, on the day after Thanksgiving 2010 (Black Friday), we were visited by Weedleman himself—unannounced, unscheduled, and unprecedented. What follows is our recollection and record of that meeting. Prior to our meeting, Weedleman was a recluse. Following our meeting Weedleman has neither appeared in any manner nor in any forum. He is assumed to be in hiding or to have ascended to the great beyond. We have resisted speculation as to his whereabouts and condition.

This is the last known communication to date granted to humanity by Buck Weedleman. It was granted to us exclusively by Weedleman. After much deliberation, we have decided to share the encounter with the public via this transcript of the "Weedleman Interviews". Go forward from here with caution and respect, for this is the word and wisdom of Weedleman.

Jacobs/Stoops

"Mr. Weedleman!" I said with an appropriate and ample level of shock, awe and surprise.

"Please call me Buck or Weedleman or Buck Weedleman." He said pleasantly, but with an element of seriousness that implied a matter-of-fact attitude that is a hallmark of most great thinkers.

"Sorry, of course, as you wish Mr. Weedleman." I said not realizing I'd addressed him in the same disagreeable fashion as before.

"Is there someone else I could talk to here?" He asked casually as if used to testing the listening ability of those around him.

Feeling cornered, I started spouting off gibberish that confused the smart and stupid alike. Given the opportunity, I can really screw things up. Despite this, I forged on. "I'm sorry. Yes, I'll get one of my fellow researchers," I said in a dejected tone, as I had just become aware of my sophomoric breach of etiquette and general inability to follow simple instruction.

"Never mind," Buck continued. "I'm used to people getting my instructions wrong. At least you caught your mistake and attempted to cure. I appreciate anyone's attempt to put things right. We all make mistakes; few of us make the effort to be accountable for those mistakes. Most people misquote me for their own purposes. These 'cons' move on to use whatever meaning they have assigned to their misquotation of me as literal and use it to their own advantage; pursuing whatever misguided agenda they desire. You didn't act with that level of culpability/ blameworthiness, so we can continue."

"Thank you, Buck," I said with my confidence restored.

"That's quite alright. I don't believe you to be culpable—inattentive or perhaps stupid, but not culpable," he said as matter—of-factly as before.

"Thank you—I guess," I replied. How do you respond to such a semi-polite, semi-rude, half non-compliment such as his characterization of me had been? I was genuinely thrilled to have him there so I pressed on, without addressing the ambivalence or indifference of my strangely interesting, yet somewhat recalcitrant visitor.

"We have some questions for you, Buck. May we interview you?"

Buck acquiesced.

"I guess the first thing that I'd like to know is, 'why us?' I'm not lacking in self confidence, but you are the most sought after subject to be interrogated. Why would you choose three researchers of limited experience to examine and divulge your thoughts & ideas?" I asked.

"Why do I tell anything to anyone is probably the better question," he responded. "No one has ever done a terrific job of telling my stories; so why NOT you? If you do a good job, that will be unique and if you screw it up, you'll be in good company."

"Fair enough," I said as I wasn't certain as to whether or not I had just been criticized or praised.

"There are a variety of things/topics that I'd like to discuss with you and get your thoughts and opinions. Is there anything in particular that you'd like to talk about?" I asked.

"I am always prepared for any topic. Ask whatever you wish," Weedleman said as though tired from enduring a lifetime of fielding shallow and inane questions framed in language designed to mimic importance.

"Thank you." I responded. "Let's get started then."

"Fair enough," said Buck playfully. I wasn't sure if he was mocking me or not—it didn't matter. Perhaps he was being sardonic, certainly acerbic, but I knew I'd better not spend too much time pondering his mental state. I needed to get on with the interview before he lost interest and vanished as quickly and as mysteriously as he had appeared.

"Many people are consumed with perfection," I started. "Is perfection a reasonable pursuit?"

"No," he responded. "Most people will never achieve perfection. Then, when they realize they can't achieve it they don't attempt to be adequate. Perfectionism is paralyzing and achieves nothing. People need to learn to embrace adequate—it's a waste of life to do anything less or more."

"I see." I responded. "Could you explain adequate to me by way of example?" I continued.

"Sure," he said. "Chris Rock once described the General Education Development (GED) certificate as the 'Good Enough Degree'. That's funny. You know what else is funny—not laugh out loud funny, but intriguing funny? The societal necessity to confirm a person's basic ability to read, write, and calculate before allowing that individual to serve in any capacity up to and including as the President of the United States (I know reading, writing, and math aren't actually requirements to become President—there are other specific requirements however, so just stay with me on this one). At the same time," Buck continued, "Society allows anyone to procreate and subsequently do as much or as little as possible to instill in their creations the basic necessities to grow into morally/ fiscally responsible, respectful, and respectable beings. There is precious little forethought given to the guidance of these creatures that will one day be the leaders of our world. The day when these creatures become our leaders will find our generation old and in failing health; we will have missed the opportunity to guide the rising generation as to the issues of waging war, striving for basic human rights, seeking justice, creating peace, developing tolerance, or engaging in basic thoughtful contemplation. As John Stuart Mill has so aptly stated:

> *[The existing generation is master both of the training and the entire circumstances of the generation to come; it cannot indeed make them perfectly wise and good, because it is itself so lamentably deficient in goodness and wisdom; and its best efforts are not always, in individual cases, its most successful ones; but it is perfectly well able to make the rising generation, as a whole, as good as, and a little better than, itself.*

> *If society lets any considerable number of its members grow up mere children, incapable of being acted on by rational consideration of distant motives, society has itself to blame for the consequences.] John Stuart Mill. On Liberty.*

I think that although there is no degree required to have a child perhaps there should be some general education provided on the topic so that we can all be 'good enough' parents. Our children will eventually grow up and run our world. I'd feel a little more comfortable if those children were given at least a prep-course addressing serious topics so that our countries don't continue to run around shooting at each other simply because that's the only solution they've ever been taught."

Buck continued, "You may wonder why I would set my sights on simply 'adequate' rather than 'superior' or 'the best' or anything greater than simply adequate when referring to parenting or any pursuit really. The answer lies in how we define adequate. Billy Joel once described himself as an adequate (or perhaps it was competent) musician. Now whether or not you think Billy Joel is an adequate musician doesn't matter. What matters is that we embrace what it is to be adequate. Adequate means good enough—the level at which no one should fall below, and while exceeding that isn't discouraged—it isn't necessary either."

"So if you are an adequate parent that is enough?" I asked.

"Of course," responded Buck with conviction. "Now if you had a great parent or currently are a great parent, that's wonderful, but unnecessary. Take, for instance, teaching your child to swim. Every kid should learn how to swim so that if they fall into an unattended pool they will at least be able to kick to the side and get out. The standard is teaching your child (or having someone else teach them) how to avoid drowning. If you'd like to train them to swim the English Channel or break Michael Phelps records, that's fine, but not necessary. Kicking to the side of the pool so you don't drown is adequate. Furthermore, if you push your kids to train for lofty goals that are essentially your goals and not theirs, you will certainly fail the adequacy test in several other dimensions of parenting."

"Could you clarify the Billy Joel and Chris Rock?" I inquired.

"Absolutely," responded Buck. "Just for the clarity of my diffident interviewer, I would consider Billy Joel an excellent song writer. If he were an excellent musician, perhaps that would detract from his song writing abilities—losing the words in a sea of beautiful melodies."

Buck went on, "Lessons to take away from this part of our conversation: (1) teach your kids to swim, (2) Billy Joel and Chris Rock are exceptional in some areas, while merely adequate in most and (3) adequate is good enough for most things. In fact, if you spend your life trying to be exceptional at those things that you really just need to be adequate at, you'll probably miss the opportunities to be exceptional at those things that are meaningful to you (i.e., song writing for Billy Joel and comedy for Chris Rock)."

"Is music important in the upbringing of a child?" I asked Buck, expecting that he would talk at great length of the dangers of straying too far from the contemplation of deep, cerebral ideas and concepts. His answer surprised me.

Buck counseled, "Introduce your kids to the music of Eddie Van Halen. I mention EVH in all my books and interviews as an attempt to be funny or to get him to comment on it in some fashion; to draw more if that's possible. I think the real reason I mention EVH is to demonstrate that someone can speak volumes without ever saying a word. Perhaps for you it isn't EVH, but rather Elvis or Snoop Dogg or Yo Yo Ma or Beethoven/Bach/Mozart. Music transcends language and advances communication in a way that we don't truly acknowledge or appreciate."

Weedleman continued, "Kids need to know that there is so much more to be communicated within the universe than will ever be contained in speech or writing. Music gives us the ability to fly ahead of where we are; to catch a glimpse of where we might go rather than dwelling on where we are, like a Bobby Kennedy notion of looking toward what we might become and saying 'Why not?" Weedleman seemed particularly convinced of the certitude of this response.

"As for the remainder of this conversation/interview," Buck stated purposefully, "I can't cover every conceivable topic—not enough time or knowledge to do that. I will provide guidelines for adequacy in parenting on a number of topics that I am familiar with or for whatever reason have some experience with. Some topics will be happy and make you laugh while others are sad and will make you cry. I honestly wish that I could just be a tireless wellspring of happiness and sunshine, but life doesn't work like that. Life operates without regard for the wellbeing of its participants. Life has no conscience. Life has no notions of right and wrong. Life doesn't care. If any caring is to exist, it must be perpetuated by humans. If we don't adequately care, then caring won't exist. Continue your interrogation of me, my friend, and for God's sake try and do an adequate job of it."

My next topic was religion. "There has been much speculation as to whether or not you are a product of science, religion, intelligent design, or perhaps an actual figure within some religion. Would you like to confirm or deny any of this speculation?" I asked.

"Not really," he responded. "To be God is to know all things, be all powerful, and be in control of all that occurs—I simply am what I am. I doubt that any of us are the products of intelligent design—whatever that may be . . . Just look around; not really overflowing with intelligence of any sort. Could be natural selection, but it's just as likely that we are the product of a playful or bored deity who's run out of things to do. Am I powerful—yes, but so are you. We all have power and if the universe is just, we will be judged on how we have used that power."

Buck continued. "As for religion in general, use it wisely and in moderation. Philippians 4:6 basically says 'Worry about nothing; pray about everything.' 1 Thessalonians 5:17 reads 'Pray without ceasing.' Philip and Thessal were an odd sort—always talking to themselves or each other. I was never quite sure who they were talking to . . . deep in prayer I suppose—cool guys though . . . and damn good bowlers. If you want a couple of damn good bowlers who are deep in prayer, I don't know where else you look—set 'um up, knock 'um down. Don't pray all the time about everything. If there is a God, he'll think you're an idiot incapable of accomplishing anything on your own.

"Do you think God watches football or baseball?" he questioned. "And if He does, does He cause touchdowns or homeruns? That was rhetorical—no. He doesn't care about football, baseball, touchdowns, or homeruns. If you see an athlete thanking God after hitting a homerun or scoring a touchdown, realize that athlete is simply vain enough to think that God is 'on his side' or superstitious enough to believe a ritualistic/talismanic bit of nonsense will curry favor with God. If I were God and some athlete asked me for a touchdown, while that very athlete existed in fortune as children go to sleep hungry and cold, I would 'drop-kick that athlete through the goal posts of life' (Bobby Bare song adaptation). Besides, as a comedian once observed (I forgot who), if God gets credit for the touchdowns, shouldn't He take responsibility for every play? 'We were doing fine, until Jesus made me fumble,'" he quipped.

"Is there a way that we should teach the rising generation to view religion?" I asked agreeing with Weedleman as I, too, was not entirely unaccustomed to this type of epistemological conformity among the masses.

"In my humble opinion," Buck continued, "this should be your strategy: To successfully be an adequate parent as it pertains to religion, simply allow a child to question what goes on around him. If you choose to believe that an omnipotent, omniscient, omnipresent super being from beyond the reaches of the universe makes everything happen and always has—fine, but expect some questions that may be worded with the vocabulary of a child, and yet strike at the very heart of what you may hold sacred. Here's where the point of what is adequate and what is unacceptable is reached. If you condemn a child for questioning the existence of God, then you will never be an adequate parent. If you truly believe what religious books have taught us, then you would reserve the highest levels of respect for the words and deeds of children or risk the wrath of an angry ruler. Children are made in God's image and have yet to do a whole lot of sinning, so if God has favorites (and I believe He does) children are probably at the top of that list. Be extremely careful how you treat them!"

"Do you have any specific political views or affiliations?" I continued.

"No," Weedleman answered. "Good is good and bad is bad, evil is evil and righteous is righteous. These qualities can hide in any corner of politics. I suggest that you adhere to the good and righteous principles that exist in every religion and resist the temptation to affiliate that pure action/direction/advice to any specific worldly religion or political paradigm. Treat others as you would have them treat you. Variants of the Golden Rule can be found in every religion. Religion can serve a useful and honorable purpose—just don't wade too far into the nonsense and dogma. Politicians often twist realities to suit their own selfish purposes—no big surprise there. Consider, for example, the Republican Party referring to itself as the party of Abraham Lincoln. While it is true that President Lincoln was a Republican, it has been contextually re-mastered to imply that Lincoln would subscribe to the ideals of the Republican Party as it exists today. I can tell you with absolute certainty that Abraham Lincoln would be neither a Democrat nor Republican in this day and age. He would avoid politics as fervently as he tried to avoid the Civil War. Lincoln sought justice; You cannot find that in politics today."

Weedleman thundered on. "Most people don't know much about anything really and even less about politics. To be a successful politician one must pander to the crowd at hand; pandering is the opposite of leadership.—not sure who said that Lincoln, Obama, Twain (Mark or Shania) or perhaps that's a Weedleman original," he added with a smile.

"Politics is much like religion," Buck continued, "in that we don't have all the answers to every question. In politics, however, if you question the status quo, you will probably just stand in isolation rather than hang in isolation as you would in religion. Actually, I'm not sure about that. Who kills more people for not believing whatever they do? I'm guessing religious nut cases kill more, but I suppose Hitler killed an absurd number of people for political purposes, so I'll have to claim ignorance on that one—only because of lack of data points, of course, since computers were not as efficient back in the days of Hitler or the Crusades. Suffice it to say that if somebody is getting killed in a ritualistic/talismanic fashion, it's most likely religion, politics, or some convoluted conflation of both."

"In the past, you have made reference to sports and athletes generally. How do you feel about sports, athletics, etc.?" I asked.

Buck quickly and unflinchingly responded, "My dad taught me the most important things about sports that I ever needed to know. He was beyond adequate when it came to sports—he was exceptional. For any of you who know my dad, this may surprise you as he never played any organized sports that I know of. He was a math teacher for most of his life—coached mathletes."

Buck continued. "You may ask then 'How was my father an exceptional sports figure in my life?' Well, have you ever been to a sporting event where some pissed off parent is in the crowd berating the referee or umpire or coach or the other team or their child's teammates or even their own child? Well, I can assure you that person was not my father. That puts him right up to exceptional straight away. I saw other kids with fathers like that. Some of those kids were so embarrassed by their parent that they ultimately grew up to hate whatever sport it was they probably loved at an earlier stage in life. If they continued on in sports, these kids often absorbed the mythology that nothing in life was ever their fault. After all, there is always a 'referee' of some type to blame for a loss. Do enough blaming and you're free to act with utter and absolute reckless disregard for others and with zero responsibility for anything that happens around you.

You don't need to practice harder or eat right and get enough rest before your game/match because you cannot be held responsible for the shortcomings of another individual's poor eyesight or bad judgment. You live a pathetic, yet carefree life. Look around your spot in the world. This happens a lot no matter where you are or who you surround yourself with. Whether at work or at play, some people blame themselves for everything, while others don't take responsibility for anything. Although I'm not sure which is worse, both groups are dangerous."

"In any event," Buck went on, "my dad let me enjoy sports as I wanted to. I owned the experience. He didn't live vicariously through me, nor did he ignore my efforts/interests. Had he done so he would have subsequently been teaching me either to live through my children, expecting my offspring to provide for me what I couldn't accomplish myself, or that discounting my children's dreams, talents and desires, while still expecting them to become confident, courageous, capable adults is perfectly acceptable. That's being a shameful coward not an empowering role model." Buck concluded the subject with, "my dad's the greatest sportsman I've ever known."

"You have been quite virulently in opposition toward sports and sports figures generally," I started. "We know from previous interviews that you have tremendous respect for Walter Payton because of his selflessness when facing death; choosing not to elevate his importance beyond those suffering around him. He fought the illness alongside those fighting against the same ailment as he was suffering. Walter chose to fight alongside his teammates around him never abandoning them to take the easy way. Is there a sport that you like or identify with?—football?"

"Yes" he replied, "but not football. I prefer golf and ultimate fighting."

"They've integrated golf and ultimate fighting?" I quipped attempting to be funny. Buck smiled at me with the mused pity you might expect from a wedding audience politely laughing at the toast of an uncomfortable, unfunny best man, or drunken relative. Buck was the kind of person who couldn't make himself laugh at a joke he'd already heard a thousand times—not even to be polite.

"No, my friend, they have yet to successfully combine the two sports—too many contradicting aphorisms. The most egregious being 'keep your head down when you swing'—necessary in golf, while a killer mistake in ultimate fighting." He said to ease the sting of my ill-advised venture into the world of comedy.

"Why do you like ultimate fighting?" I asked assuming him to be a generally peaceful being.

"It's one of the few sports that have an intrinsic honesty about it," he replied. "There is purity in knowing that when some muscle-bound MMA fighter hits someone that they go unconscious. If you want truth, there you have it. It is brutal for sure, but true—much like life. Life doesn't wear boxing gloves or hit you with a breakaway folding chair or let you get prepared with protective gear before it attacks. Life is a muscle-bound MMA fighter swinging wildly at a specific target yet hitting with precision and power when it does get focus. The reality of life doesn't wear boxing gloves or ring a bell informing you when to expect your first concussion-laced blow—it just hits you when it feels like it on its terms—reckless, ruthless, random, and relentless."

"Well that was, well . . . depressing," I said. "Maybe you like golf a bit better?"

"Yes" replied Buck. "Golf is like ultimate fighting in its honesty, but rarely do you get knocked unconscious. The sport of golf allows for redemption. You can have an awful round, yet you are allowed one good shot that keeps you coming back. The redemption of that one good shot makes you want to keep swinging through the awful rounds so as to again savor those few redeeming shots. Within the game is the motivation to pursue the occasional 'perfect' shot and in so pursuing that 'perfect' shot your entire game gets better. That is like life. We will all fail, but we will succeed as well. The beauty in life, like golf, is that it isn't ruled by the things that make you despise it. Rather, its beauty is found in the things that keep you coming back to it to get better."

Buck continued, "Golf allows you the opportunity to simultaneously experience predictability and disarray. If routine brings security then disarray breeds ingenuity—golf provides a playful combination of both. Within the game of golf exists the freedom to dream beyond where you are while remaining in a comfortable place."

"Do you like the idea that sports are integrated into smaller localities?" I continued, "Should children be involved in sports? Is there something they can learn from the experience?"

Buck took his time and answered reluctantly, "500 years from now there will be operas performed about the local sports dramas of this era. Ostensibly local sporting groups are designed around teaching children of all skill levels to enjoy healthy competition and sportsmanship. In reality, local sporting groups are a dramatic mix of good intentions, poor execution, and the successful demonstration of pseudo diplomacy that makes the United Nations look tame."

Annoyed, Buck pressed on. "In the abstract, children's leagues are a perfect forum to demonstrate to school age kids exactly what to expect in the spectacle of life—a series of teachable moments. As it turns out the whole process of pushing sports onto the children of today is a teachable moment with respect to the level of dysfunction adults bring upon themselves and then pass on to the next generation. Children are taught to expect that when someone says something driven solely by emotion, they will later find it followed up by a rationalization to convince themselves and whomever they surround themselves with that they acted civilly and in the best interest of all those involved—most notably the children. Yes—the children."

Weedleman continued, "Children are the 'kickstand' that keeps the motorcycle of local sporting from losing all credibility and balance. Without that kickstand the bike falls to the ground resting lifelessly on the asphalt of parental missed opportunities, personal compromise, and the vicarious pursuit of greatness. With the kickstand propping up the notion that what children learn is virtue of the highest order, we as post-prime athletic hangers-on can press on with the in-fighting, name calling, back stabbing, sophomoric threats, and, of course, fund raising."

"Could we teach our children better than this? I asked.

"Of course!" Buck shot back obviously agitated.

"Is it likely that we will?" I pressured.

"Of course not," Weedleman continued. "People want to keep that motorcycle upright and balanced, even if it is on the backs of the children. Let me give you one glaring example of the sad spectacle inherent in local sports before I let this topic go. There are good coaches and fans out there. This anecdote does not include any of those good people. It's a time consuming and generally thankless job—and there are a precious few out there that do it to improve the children. Society's gratitude should go out to them."

Buck continued with his example. "Here's a thoroughly contemptible demonstration of some thoroughly pathetic people—I hope you find them as cowardly and weak as I do. I grew up in Illinois—about 100 miles outside of Chicago. I lived in a place dotted with small communities that were very enthusiastic about their local sports teams. Sounds good so far, right? Wait for the idiocracy to reveal itself (an idiocracy is a society in which the most idiotic of the group are elevated to levels of distinction and leadership). The reality of some of these communities is that they were over-flowing with idiots. Two of these communities that were teeming (no pun intended—maybe intended—not sure) with idiots found themselves in a state football showdown. The game was tied—the clock running down—the fans drunk. A perfect setting for the crowd to usurp the children's time in the limelight . . . and that's what happened."

"This doesn't sound too extreme." I interrupted.

"May I continue?" said Buck with a dark sarcasm almost as vitiating with me as he had been with the local idiots he had just referenced. "A referee made a bad call, after which the locals got into a pissing match over the whole thing, even going to the paper to editorialize on the bad call. The referee later acknowledged the bad call and even apologized to the local idiots. That wasn't enough for the idiocracy. Instead of teaching kids to accept an imperfect world or to try to take realistic steps to better the world, the local idiots went on the attack calling for the referee to step down (quit)."

Buck paused with sadness and anger at what he was to say next. "The referee killed himself. More accurately, the idiots of these two communities drove this innocent child of someone to suicide. Congratulations idiots—I hope your children get away from you soon and never return. Your moronic little litter-box communities have really done enough. If you happen to be one of these people who drove this person to suicide. Please be reasonable and take that same drive yourself—loser!" he said disgustedly, pausing reflectively to take a drink, hoping to once again remove that despicable memory, at least from the forefront of his cognition."

After a moment, I pressed on. "Very little is known about your academic background. Are academics important?" I asked.

"Of course," Buck replied, "but only if academics are defined as learning. I've known many people who have attained very formal & impressive degrees, but learned very little in the process. I really don't consider that to be academic excellence. Einstein said that education is what remains after you forget everything that you learned in school. Maybe he's right—I don't know. I am certain that there are few moments in life that don't offer the opportunity to learn. If we can agree that academics should be equated with learning then you can learn virtually anywhere at any time. I have had dreams that have caused me to think far beyond what is offered in a typical classroom. So, have I pursued academics while asleep? If academics are equated with learning then, yes, I should have a degree in "sleepology". And if you can allow yourself to soak in that idea, so should you. Sleep is where the mind asks the questions and seeks the answers that are truly meaningful to you specifically. Everyone should "major" in becoming themselves anyway. Everything else you know should be used simply as an adjunct to develop who you are. To address your question directly, I continue to work in pursuit of my degree toward adequately becoming Buck Weedleman."

Moving on I asked, "Do you have an economic preference—capitalism, socialism, or communism?"

Buck followed with "All economic approaches are perfect in the abstract. It's the practical application of them to society that makes them useful or destructive. I like what works—probably somewhere between capitalism and socialism. Pure capitalism exists only in the mob (organized crime). If you think you're truly a free marketeer then nothing is off limits—collusion, extortion, all manner of violence—the mob. Meanwhile, pure socialism winds up taking from those who have until you run out of those who have—I think Margaret Thatcher said that. People should be driven by their ability to excel for personal gain, but children shouldn't ever—ever—have to go to bed cold and hungry because we are afraid to tax the excesses of another. There is a level at which no one should fall below. You can call that socialism if you like. I call it moral responsibility."

"Regardless of what you said earlier about your perceived position in any or all religions, including science, Buck, you are a religious figure of sorts," I said, stepping back into the portentous topic of religion. "You are spoken of often on the fringes of religious communities. Here is some of what has been written about you in the religious press:"

"In the beginning there was Buck Weedleman. Buck was lonely so he created fish. The fish were boring to Buck so he created dogs. The dogs ran away so he created giraffes. Buck found the giraffes to be weird so he set out creating things left and right as his discontent continued. So if you venture out into the universe today and find yourself perplexed by a strange creature, don't ruminate on its purpose in the grand scheme of things, since it likely doesn't have one. Buck Weedleman created many creatures that serve absolutely no purpose. These creatures or critters are the simple result of what happens when a great deity becomes lonesome and bored."

"Does Buck Weedleman know everything? Has he created everything?" I asked.

"Maybe," Buck responded. "Am I all-knowing, all-powerful, and ever-present? I think so, but I don't really know for sure. I'm a bit like a calculus teacher. The teacher understands many complex relationships, but (a) struggles to impart what he knows to his students and (b) struggles to take his knowledge beyond where it is. Like I said, I don't know if I know everything, but I do know that I look with sadness on those whom I cannot teach. Perhaps the greatest pain isn't borne by the student taught to diffuse the bomb, but rather by the teacher who must exist within a universe in which some of his students will never be able to diffuse that bomb. The teacher will suffer the unrelenting and intrusive question of whether or not he was an adequate enough teacher or if the bomb was simply beyond his knowledge. Either way, the student is gone and all that remains is uncertainty, sadness and the memory of the promising light within that student that continues to radiate within our minds and within the elusive energy that is life."

"While I don't know exactly what you know, Buck, or who you coach/teach/counsel, I am confident that you're trying. You are anything but lazy. What do you attempt to teach your typical 'student'?" I asked.

Buck responded, "I, much like you and everyone else, struggle with the complexities that I've woven myself into. Like most of us, I do what I see as necessary and important. Honestly, who isn't conflicted about what they 'should' be doing? I suppose that I could give all my money to charity & that sounds like an act of pure goodness, but haven't I just created another poor family by my act of charity? Doesn't it make more sense to pull someone from the raging river than to jump in with them? Maybe I'm just trying to find a way to get everyone out of the river rather than jumping in and having all hope swept away. Much like the anguish felt by Holden Caulfield in the Catcher in the Rye, as he was trying to keep the children from running through the field to death or some difficult to describe, yet certain oblivion."

Buck continued, "I think that I get in the most trouble when I become convinced that I'm absolutely right—I've never been absolutely right. Conflicted by the prospect of having to choose between what people should do and what they should not do, I think that I will leave that decision mostly up to them. I like to think that I just provide suggestions; suggestions that can be considered and discarded or utilized, but ultimately left for the individual to accept or reject of their own free will/volition. Disentangling myself from things I've said relating to what others should or should not do has proven again and again to be a particularly challenging endeavor. If I feel that I have pushed someone in the wrong direction, I then tend to find myself trying to un-ring a bell that I have imprudently rung; I find myself digging myself deeper and deeper into a pit of regrettable missteps and misstatements that could have been easily avoided by letting someone make their own decisions. At the same time I hate to see someone fall off Holden Caulfield's rye field if I think I can help them; an unsettling position to be in."

"Buck, as a revered figure in many religious circles, can you comment on how you see the human species fitting in to the universe at large?" I asked.

"Sure," Buck responded. "The human species is forever caught between what they are, what they want to be, and what they believe they can become. The distinction between humans in this regard is that some patiently wait for their "ship to come in" while others pursue the place to which they believe themselves entitled to be—often with self-destructive reckless abandon."

"How does the human species fit into the universe?" I asked.

"I'm not sure you want to ask that question." Buck retorted.

"Why?" I asked.

"Original sin," responded Weedleman.

"What?" I responded with obvious confusion.

"You know—original sin, eating from the tree of knowledge, flirting with disaster in the Garden of Eden." Buck went on.

"Please explain how these concepts relate to the human species as they fit into the universe," I requested with a curious irony not lost on either of us.

"Fine, but this is given to you of your own volition—your free will—your . . ." Buck started.

"Wonderful—I'll sign a waiver . . ." I tersely interrupted. "Just tell me how the human species fits into the universe . . . in your opinion."

Buck leaned back, looked up as if focusing on something that wasn't there, took a breath and started into a story as though it were taken directly from the tree of knowledge. "Stephen Hawking was once asked what one question he would ask a Supreme Being if he ever found himself in that situation. Hawking said that he would inquire as to why there is something instead of nothing. This curiosity resonates with many people. You are either drawn to that question or you think it superfluous. That is the dividing line in the human species and the defining characteristic or line of demarcation between the human species in the universe and the rest of the universe. Humans have the capacity to question why. Not all humans take advantage of the ability to ask why, but for the grace of God do they go on. Every human has the opportunity to either accept what happens to them without question or to seek an explanation behind it. Stated differently, some people will happily eat from the rest of the garden without ever approaching the forbidden fruit; while others will question why it is that the forbidden fruit is forbidden. The happy group just accepts; doesn't question; simply follows orders; 'Ours is not to reason why. Ours is but to do or die'—Alfred Lord Tennyson. The curious, on the other hand—well, we know what happened to the cat."

"So why the harsh treatment of the curious while the not so curious go on by the grace of God?" I asked.

"The treatment is disparate because the curious chose to ask a question that even God struggles with," Buck responded.

"What is the question that even God struggles with?" I asked.

"What is absolute knowledge and truth?" Buck replied.

"I thought that He would have that one nailed (no pun intended) by now," I stated quizzically.

Buck continued. "God knows what He knows; just like the rest of us. He may know everything, but He can't be sure. To assume you know everything is irresponsible at best; God is at least responsible. The warning from God against the partaking of the forbidden fruit is not to protect us from Him, but rather to protect us from the misery that may accompany the knowledge that we may acquire through our own curiosity. Perhaps there are some questions that are better left unasked. 'Be careful what you wish for cause you just might get it all and then some you don't want.'—Chris Daughtry."

Weedleman went on for some time:

> *If it helps, think about it this way; suppose you're having a dream. Within the confines (or expanses) of your dream, you see a doorway in the distance. The doorway*

is close enough so that you can hear unrecognizable yet audible sounds from it. You are also able to see light coming from the doorway in a fashion that one might attribute to a television set that has been left on.

Further within your dream consider that no one is with you that you know of and it is dark, isolated, and desolate. The only point of reference in your surroundings is the doorway. You are drawn to it yet cautious as dreams can hold torment and terror within them just as easily as they can contain beauty, bliss, knowledge, and enlightenment.

Perhaps if you choose to approach the doorway it will welcome you to a panacea of unimagined reward and pleasure. However, the doorway could house all the pain and anguish that your imagination can contrive. Maybe the doorway just leads to another room with more mystery and little else.

Maybe if you go through the door you will never be the same way again—in a good way; or perhaps you will be exposed to things that will scar you for life, leaving you with nothing short of the personality paralyzing effects of post traumatic stress disorder (PTSD).

It's your dream. You can do what you want. I wouldn't make that decision for you even if I were God. If you stay in God's 'garden', He will take care of you. If you leave the 'garden', He can't make any promises.

Religious people generally hate this idea because it paints their God as less than perfect. The trouble with placating one religion by adopting their beliefs is that you alienate other religions that may have the same good intentions and the same artifacts and history based tales of how the world works. This is where the peace that is espoused by virtually every religion starts to break down. Basically people operate from the standpoint that other religions are fine so long as they are subservient to their own religion. Once a conflict is established, the religion's 'warriors' fight it out in a 'might makes right' duel that gives new meaning to the terms war, peace, tolerance, and revulsion.

So if you want to see what's on the other side of that door, you have to make that decision yourself. While life may seem easier by just letting the forbidden fruit alone, life is then, by definition, a life without knowledge. I've never been an advocate of blind adherence to what someone else says. I like to have some logical basis for what I believe. Make your choice as to whether or not you go through the 'dream door' wisely as I have never been a fan of PTSD either.

"Have you experienced any tragedy in your life?" I asked.

"Tragedy visits every house eventually, and I have not been able to hide from it." Weedleman continued, "Tragedy brings out the best in some people, the worst in others, and the stupidity in most." He went on with a quote. "Abraham Lincoln once quipped that a person should only speak if they could improve upon silence. Strangely, it seems that the collective conversation within society is led by those most ill-equipped to improve upon silence. It is not my intent to try and silence the voices within the world generally. We all are enlightened to a certain extent and should speak up from time to time as is the case with the example I have set myself and more so through the ample selective verbal offerings given by countless others throughout history."

Buck reflected, "A teacher once told me that the greatest strength of a lawyer is not the ability to grasp the facts and make the perfect argument, but rather, the ability to process information and form reasonable arguments while talking around an issue—the ability to dance around an issue just far enough to remain relevant, but not so close to the truth to really be saying anything. If we break that tactic down a bit, it's the ability to speak without saying anything—in vain—as the wind blows—having perfect form and no substance. Speaking without saying anything is a gift. We all have this gift to a certain degree, but we are usually unaware of when we are using it."

Buck went on, "How does this relate to tragedy? Well, tragedy happens—that's just part of our reality. What we need to understand and respect is the fact that no remark is lost on someone who has suffered a tragic event in life. If you have ever endured a tragedy (and you probably have) you can probably recall seemingly innocuous comments from others that cut you to the core. I remember a fairly common comment made when our family had a stillborn child, 'He's in a better place now.' I know that the comment was meant to comfort us, but it failed on nearly every level except what was intended by the sympathizer. I'm a fairly literal person. When someone says that my dead son is now in a better place than he would have been had he lived & been with me and my family, all I heard was how awful life would have been for my wonderful child had he been forced to exist with and among his family in our home. I'm literal and that's all I heard."

Buck reflected with focused sorrow, "When a child is lost, continuity is lost when form is forced. You can force yourself to believe anything you choose, but it will fly in the face of reason and reality. The perfect circle (perfect order) probably exists, but worldly/conventional religion has yet to produce it. Without perfection, religion is 49% good intentions, 49% cruel intentions, 1% truth, and 1% fairy tale."

"Buck, what religion do you practice?" I asked.

"I really don't know what religion I am," he said, "or if I ever practiced a specific one. I spend most of my life actually helping people in a tangible, empirical, measurable fashion—feeding the hungry—housing the homeless—clothing the naked. I guess I am more of a food, shelter, and clothing type guy, rather than a purveyor of any particular ideology. Perhaps I am a 'Do unto others as you would have them do unto you' type person. As I said earlier, that golden rule is found in most religions. Unfortunately, I'm not sure if it ever gets the priority attention it should. Religions, like lawyers, tend to dwell on small details (Don Henley) or fiddle while Rome burns (Nero)."

"So base your religions on service to those in need (food, shelter, & clothing) until that perfect circle is discovered or revealed. Perhaps there is only a journey with the destination, living inextricably within the journey, bound to that journey, existing forever as a dream to keep us moving toward a better place, individually and collectively. Perhaps God only exists in helping others. Perhaps that is Truth. Religion should follow truth and not the other way around. God is Truth. Truth is helping others as we would want to be helped (food, shelter, & clothing). Until we practice the basics of helping one another, we will never even be remotely close to Truth/perfection/ God," concluded Weedleman.

"Why are some people afforded many great talents while others are forever struggling?" I asked.

"I really don't know much about why one person can jump four feet in the air and another can't move their legs at all," retorted Buck. "Don't you think that we should allow for both to exist within society? At least until we have a better grasp of the situation? And while we're at it, could we acknowledge the value of the individual by acknowledging the cost of their care? People who can't walk don't need Wesley Matthews or Michael Jordan type money or vertical jump, but the basic expectations of you & I should not be inconceivable for someone with special needs. Again, there is a level at which no one should fall below," he asserted shaking his head dejectedly.

Buck fired angrily, "I read stuff like this from people like me all the time. When will we make it a reality? We have tapped all that we can out of current intelligence. We must look for different perspectives—different cognitive approaches. We must look to the next generations for those perspectives/cognitive approaches as ours are painfully deficient in problem solving techniques and abilities. Tell the rising generations what we know and then get out of their way. We can't keep traveling down the same path we have been. If the definition of insanity is doing the same thing over and over again always expecting a different result then we are all insane. The only rational response to an insane world is, perhaps, individual insanity, but the level of irrational behavior among the world's participants has become alarming—alarmist as it sounds, we are losing control of all that surrounds us. We need fresh blood with better ideas; tell them what we know, get out of their way, and hope for the best."

"Are you afraid of anything?" I asked.

"Of course," Buck continued, "in the words of Fred G. Sanford, I am afraid of 'Bees & Disease'"

"I do recall an account of one of your followers from some years ago regarding bees," I said. "It went something like this:"

The wisdom of Weedleman could not be interrupted . . . much. He was fairly focused and passionate about the state of the universe and the human condition. He was, however, not completely immune from the fears of ordinary humans. His fears were both rational and irrational. He could be in the midst of taking the wisdom of Weedleman to a whole new level when he would get distracted by a bee. Yes—a bee.

Was he allergic to bees? No. He was a bee coward. You may think it a bit bold of me to refer to Buck Weedleman as a coward in any respect, but the truth compels me to stick to the facts—he was 'yella' when it came to bees.

I'm afraid of bees to a certain extent. I suppose we all are bee cowards on some level, but Buck could see one sweat bee in the window of a gymnasium and immediately run for cover. As a follower of this 'visionary', it was a bit embarrassing. One minute he'd have a room full of strangers ready to lay down their lives for him & the next moment he'd be running like a six year old girl from "A bee! A bee!" There really is no regaining control of a crowd after your speaker flees the scene based on the presence of a disinterested insect. I would be the first (well, the second behind

Buck) to run from a swarm of killer bees protecting their queen, but honestly, a sweat bee? Embarrassing.

"It's nice of you to bring up this part of my reality," Buck said in a playfully sarcastic way.

"Sorry," I continued, "So bees are the irrational fear while disease was the more reality based fear?"

"Yes, all people fear disease," responded Buck. "Even people who generally have a reckless disregard for their own safety, typically have a fear of disease. Why?—Because they lack control over disease. I may be reckless with the way I live, but I'd like to choose the risks I take. A disease dictates what fight you will fight on its own terms for as long as it wishes to fight with you. It's a bit like having a tornado pick up your house from wherever it is and throw it down somewhere else—destroying most of your stuff in the process. You know tornados exist, but you never really expect to get hit by one. It's a fairly random event that threatens your existence, when the odds were on your side that it wouldn't affect you at all."

Buck continued, "Disease incorporates a fairness aspect to it that makes us feel cheated. It always amazes me how everything we think about ourselves is relative to our surroundings. When our son died (stillbirth) I felt cheated, then 2 weeks later, friends of ours lost a son who was only 4. Now what am I supposed to think? How am I supposed to feel? I'll give you the short answer on this one—don't compare unfair events. Don't get caught up in the losing game of comparative grief. Most people feel lost & depressed after a tragedy. Does it really matter if you are the most lost and depressed? There is no award for 'Most Lost and Depressed'. Besides, what joy in victory if your story is sadder than mine? We're both sad and depressed. How is there a 'winner' within this scenario? There isn't."

Buck went on, "Disease is a cheat to you while you're in the general population, then you go to a disease facility (hospital) and you all of a sudden see people in worse shape than you are, and then you feel guilty for feeling cheated. Don't play this game—everyone at the hospital was cheated."

Buck reflected on hospitals. "I once took one of my sons to the University of Wisconsin's Children's Hospital after he broke his arm during a football game when he was 12 years old. I speeded to the hospital—going through stoplights—laying down a string of profanity that was probably a personal record even for me. When we got to the hospital, I was complaining about the parking, the time of day, the angle of the Earth's axis, you name it I was complaining about it. I was perplexed and angered with regard to this universal conspiracy that had befallen my son and our family. Then I got into the hospital. As far as level of injury goes, nearly every other patient in that hospital would have traded whatever they had for a broken arm."

Weedleman continued, "I underwent an amazing transformation; an epiphany, if you will. While at the football stadium/field where he was injured, we were the most unlucky of all those present. Then, minutes later, when we arrived at the children's hospital, we were the luckiest people in the building."

As if still in awe of the hospital, Buck said, "The UW Children's Hospital was/is the most amazing/Beautiful/miraculous place that I have ever been to—yet I hope that I never have to see the inside of that beautiful place again. If you think that you've been cheated in life, I suggest you visit a children's hospital and re-evaluate your current condition."

"How should the world help children with special needs?" I asked.

Buck replied, "First, every child has special needs. If we considered every child special then this part of our talk would be unnecessary. I wish this part of our conversation was superfluous; however, we rarely treat anyone as special, so I must continue on with this topic."

If you are tempted to skip this part of the conversation because you don't have a child with traditional special needs, I encourage you not to. The problems that you have relating to your child may be addressed here.

Buck pressed on. "I don't even know what the definition of a special needs child is. I'm guessing that it hinges on the degree to which a child deviates from the average child. I don't know what an average child is either. The implication with these definitions is that we would like every child to be average? Is that what anyone wants?"

Buck continued, "For the sake of simplicity, let's define children with special needs as those who require more time and resources to accomplish basic tasks within society than does the "average" child. Requiring more time and resources equals special."

Weedleman proceeded, "The choice with this is simple: you either see a person as deserving of extra time and resources or you don't. That's a choice that says far more about you than the person that deviates from average."

"I used to be able to dunk a basketball," said Buck. "I can't anymore. I recently had the good fortune to meet Wesley Matthews (NBA star). He was putting on a free basketball clinic for young (middle school—high school) basketball players. Two of my kids attended this clinic. Again the clinic was free, just so you know what a good guy Wesley Matthews is."

Buck continued to drive the lane. "Wesley Matthews can dunk a basketball. I can't. In fact, in this world most people can't dunk a basketball. Does that make Wesley Matthews special? Should we try to make him more 'average' like the rest of us? You may be thinking that what Wesley Matthews has is a talent not a special need. What I can assure you is that Wesley Matthews requires more time and resources from society—about 6 or 7 million dollars a year. Does he deviate from average? Yes. Does he require more resources from society? Yes. By my definition he has special needs."

Buck poignantly summed up, "My point here is that in a world of unique individuals—"average" is just a concept, never a reality. We should celebrate those of us needing extra resources. Why? Because we have only a vague notion of what differentiates Wesley Matthews from someone in a wheelchair."

"Could you tell us more about education or intelligence generally?" I asked.

"Certainly," Weedleman responded. "Here's a take on intelligence—consider a combination lock that has 100 numbers required to open it. One person may have 80 of those numbers another may have 19 and another only one—the person with 80 numbers would seem more important, but aren't they all equally necessary to open the lock? Intelligence is the same in that one person may know many things, but may never have enough knowledge to truly ever figure anything out in an absolute sense—at least not without the knowledge of the others for sure."

Weedleman continued, "An adequate parent encourages a child to get 'B's'. This begs the question, 'Why not 'A's'? Well this notion is based on the teaching of Professor Dudley Riggle, a college professor of mine. Dr. Riggle once told our class that the best students he had got B's because they were paying enough attention to take an interest in a topic to the extent that they would miss some information on subsequent topics, so when those subsequent topics would show up on the next test they would miss them and get B's. The 'A' students simply regurgitated facts while never really thinking through to a higher level."

Buck hesitated, and then continued, "You may dismiss this as nonsense & it may, in fact, be nonsense, but think about medical school for a minute. No one has cured cancer yet. So if I go to any medical school in the world and get straight A's, learning everything they know, I won't have the cure for cancer. Cancer will never be cured by an 'A' student. It will take a 'B' or perhaps a 'C' student to knock that one out."

"The "B" student will hear something during a lecture or see something during an experiment and say, 'That just isn't right'," said Buck. "From there they will follow their curiosity to a cure while half the class gets better grades than they do. Does anyone know the grade point average (GPA) that Jonas Salk had? No. He developed the polio vaccine so no one cares about his GPA. Maybe it was a 3.1 or so—doesn't matter—curing polio was really the big thing for Jonas."

"Do you have any specific thoughts on death?" I asked.

"Generally I'm against it," Weedleman started, "Death happens and so far we can't stop it. Maybe we truly don't want to be able to stop it. Maybe, just like a kid playing a video game we want to do everything on this level and then move to the next."

"That sounds a bit depressing." I continued. "Does Buck Weedleman ever get depressed?" I asked.

"Of course," he responded, "but I've always had this advice for my children, 'Don't get depressed. No matter how f'd up your life may become, it isn't worth getting depressed over.' I derived most of this wisdom from a book called 'Night' by Elie Weisel in which he discusses his experiences in a Nazi concentration camp. He ultimately decides that the only thing that can't be taken from you is how you choose to feel about something."

Buck went on, "The only thing that you truly have control over is how you choose to feel about what happens to you. This paradigm is very profound and empowering, especially considering the backdrop to which he (Elie Weisel) came to this conclusion.

"Ruminating on the positive = euphoria

Ruminating on the negative = depression

Walking between them = sanity"

"Do you have any other thoughts about death?" I asked.

Buck reflected a moment then replied, "Some topics I discuss are ones in which I wish I had absolutely no experience whatsoever—this is one of them. Being an adequate parent means going through difficult family times with your children. When my two oldest kids (I have five altogether) were 6 & 8 years old they lost a brother. As I mentioned earlier, we had a stillborn child at 38 weeks into pregnancy."

Buck continued with a strangely calm reticence, "I must admit that I don't really know what constitutes adequate parenting in this situation. Most of the things that I think I did adequately were either done without any active thinking (done on auto-pilot) or were done at the suggestion of others (nurses primarily)."

"Are there things that you'd like people to understand with regard to the generation that continues to exist after we are gone?" I asked.

"Certainly, however I am sadly lacking in the knowledge many will require," Buck was quick to respond. "I am happy to address issues that have arisen with my own children. I don't offer any advice relative to situations that I am unfamiliar with. At first, I thought that I would apologize for not having enough knowledge or experience to address every situation that one may be confronted with as a parent. At that point, however, a chill of reality sets in—I don't want the knowledge or experience to address every childhood issue."

Buck elaborated. "My brother and I were once going to the Mayo Clinic in Rochester, MN to visit an uncle who was dying of cancer (from smoking). We were not talking about anything in particular, but I remember that I asked if the Mayo Clinic had a Ronald McDonald House (RMH) affiliated with it. I don't recall if they do or not—what I do remember was his summation of Ronald McDonald Houses. He said that they were absolutely wonderful places that he hoped he would never have to see—my same view of the Children's Hospital in Madison, WI. A Ronald McDonald House provides for families who have sick children battling awful diseases."

Buck continued, "It is with no regret whatsoever that I cannot enlighten you with experiences from an RMH. I know some families who have lost children at various ages. I have spoken about our son, Zandyr, periodically throughout this chat and throughout my life. I will offer this general advice about how to deal with the loss of a child; realize that whatever happened is unfair and that with time a "new normal" may be reached to allow the family some sense of peace. Other than that I would suggest talking with people who have lost children. I would expound on the issue more, as I can speak for hours about just about anything, but this topic I can never make myself get too close to.

Maybe this is evidence of cowardice. I tend to think that it is probably just a survival skill that prevents me from truly trying to put myself in the shoes of someone who has lost a 4 year old, a 25 year old, a 39 year old, etc. I apologize, but anything I've ever tried to say or write about this falls well short of being helpful—just know that I wish you peace."

Weedleman continued, "My best advice for dealing with the loss of a child is to acknowledge the existence and meaning of the child. I recently listened to an author of a famous book talk about the true meaning of the book. He said that an author can decide what to write, but only the reader can decide what it means. The same holds true when a life ends. I can lead my life in such a way that I ultimately declare that I was good or bad or constructive or destructive, but really the summation of my life lies in the judgment of others, not in my own perception."

"Much is the same with losing a child," continued Buck, "perhaps even more acutely, at least in my experience, with the loss of a child you never had a chance to know. I recall holding and looking at my lost child for long periods of time and just wondering what would have been and probably more persistently wondering why the game ended here, seemingly, before it began."

"In a way our little mystery man was just that—a mystery novel in which you are never allowed to read the last few pages. He was the author of a story that would be given meaning by those who heard about him, but he would never be there to complete the story for you," Buck offered with a vacant distant stare.

"I spoke earlier about religion, saying that it should be used wisely and in moderation," Weedleman continued, "then I went on to denigrate sports figures who 'thank God' for touchdowns and homeruns. Sports figures are by in large a pathetic bunch who shouldn't be listened to on any topic."

Buck rebounded exuberantly "There are a few exceptions to this rule. As I mentioned earlier, Walter Payton is really the only one that comes to mind. Walter Payton had the resources to get an organ transplant without waiting in line with the rest of humanity. He chose to judge himself as an equal to those suffering his same unfair fate. He died awaiting a transplant. If you've been looking for a real hero in this confusing era of demagogues, I highly recommend Walter Payton; a genuine hero in a world in which the term hero is cast onto virtually anyone, whether or not they are deserving of it."

Buck continued "I think that perhaps the only religious experience I've had occurred in the early morning of Monday, August 30, 2004. Our son, Zandyr, was stillborn on Sunday, August 29, 2004. Our family stayed in the hospital with his shell as we referred to his body. I woke up early on the 30th and the sun was up—perfect, bright, low in the Eastern horizon soon to be eclipsed by a thick line of clouds that would persist the rest of the day. I held Zandyr in the sun's warm light. Our Zandyr looked like the rest of our kids did when they were babies. The difference was measured in degrees not appearance. The warm blood of life didn't flow through him. He was a beautiful tragedy that put me as close to the life beyond as I have ever gotten. I held my beautiful boy close to me. And in the morning sunshine, he warmed up and we were briefly together, transcending all the confusion of life. We were off on the sun-danced horizon, beyond the reach of sadness, grief, and the world's Monday morning indifference. We were free & that's as close to God as I ever want to be. For me, God doesn't show up for touchdowns and homeruns. He shows up with 5 minutes of sunshine. This is as close to God as I have ever been & it is as close to me as anyone will ever get."

Buck continued with a renewed sense of purpose. "As harsh as the reality of losing a child is, it did one thing for me that I am morosely grateful for. It made me see better my other children. I no longer wished for anything for them except to appreciate every second I am allowed to be in their sun-bright presence. When I start to get annoyed or short-tempered with them, I always remember that I never got a chance to be annoyed or short-tempered with Zandyr and I find myself back in that sun-drenched sky happily racing through the universe."

"Do you have any other thoughts regarding your other children?" I asked.

"If given the chance, I do enjoy talking about all my children," he responded, "so I guess I'll share a little bit more about them. None of the thoughts I share here concerning my kids or parents or spouse or friends could ever be all-inclusive. No single comment could cover the person in their entirety. That would be impossible. I don't know everything about them & can't pretend to sum up their existence in a few paragraphs. Having stated that, let me start with Isaiah, my first child, and finish with my fifth, Buck, Jr.:

Isaiah looks the most like me or at least what I looked like at his current age of 14 years. For many of you "age 14" was all that is necessary to understand where I'm at with my early teenager. I'm sure whatever assumptions you made are accurate to a certain extent.

Isaiah has left the 'little buddy' age and is entering the 'challenge the veracity of anything anyone else says' age. I like the little buddy age better, but if I didn't have a child that eventually challenged commonly held beliefs, I would have someone else's child—no matter how much he may look like me.

Isaiah is concerned about the nature of the world. He is sensitive to the injustices of the world. I hesitate to use the term "sensitive" because the connotation tends to be that of a weepy, sad figure, who is in a constant state of paralyzed worry regarding the human condition. Isaiah's not much like that. His 'sensitivity' towards injustice usually manifests itself in anger. I have a photograph of Isaiah looking at his lost brother, Zandyr, at the hospital. Yes, there are tears in his eyes, but they aren't tears of sadness. They are tears of anger and frustration.

They weren't tears that evidenced a feeling of 'This is so sad.' They were tears of 'There must be someone responsible for this injustice & I intend to find that person and rip their lungs out.' So that's what I can tell you about my oldest superhero, Isaiah. He is intolerant of injustice as we all should be. He's many things, but too much for this book to contain—so next up—Eli.

My 2nd son, Eli, is fearless. By fearless I don't mean that he throws rocks at lions or anything stupid like that. I mean that he really isn't concerned with what the result will be of doing something that he sees as necessary or important. By way of example, he was once playing 7th grade tackle football and taking dance lessons at the same time. I suggested that maybe he should keep the dance lesson reality quiet on the football field. He responded with, "Why? What are they going to do about it?" I really don't think that he was really insinuating that he would strike fear into the heart of anyone stupid enough to make fun of him. I think he simply was pointing out the fact that he wouldn't let the opinion of someone else, derail his life, especially when the opinion was obviously that of envy. In essence, someone who makes fun of me because I play football and dance is probably suffering with the reality that they can't do either—so how is that Eli's problem? It's not. I wish I were more like all my kids, but the fearless interpretation that others attack in an effort to hide their own weakness is something I wish I could drag into my own life a little more.

I covered what I see in the existence of Zandyr earlier. As a general recap, he's really the only one that makes me believe that there might be a God. I do think Zandyr knows where I am, what I worry about & to an extent that he watches over me. Maybe our roles switched when he died. Perhaps he watches over me like a father watches over a son, despite the fact that he is my son and I his father—stranger things have happened.

I can't move from Zandyr to Lennon without including something I wrote the day Lennon was conceived. It's about two brothers meeting each other beyond existence on earth, but not completely absent from life. One brother is on his way to earth and the other has just left the grasp of the earth:

> *I came into this life; I thought about it; I did what I could for it then I left it.*

> *I danced with my mother the most. I danced with my dad and brothers as well. I danced with my grandparents, my aunts, my uncles, my cousins, & my family's friends. My relationship with everyone was a dance. Some were awkward. Some were beautiful. Some slow, some fast, some long, some short, some driven by rage, some driven by madness, some driven by compassion, some meaningful, some meaningless . . .*

> *The problem with my dance was that it was too short. I never had time to take the floor, to speak out, to laugh, to scream, to hug, to argue, to learn, to fight, to win, to lose, to fall in love, to be disappointed, to be a disappointment, to make people laugh and smile, to be proud, to make someone proud of me . . . Did I have meaning? Perhaps, I did dance with many people.*

> *I tried to contact you. I was afraid that you couldn't hear me. I was afraid I'd forget you. I was afraid you'd forget me. I saw you cry for me and I felt better, not because you were crying, but because I could see that I*

still had meaning. I needed the sadness to keep me alive and meaningful.

I was frustrated. In my frustration I looked to others. They, too, were frustrated. They all had danced as well. Their dances had come to an end as well. They, too, took a selfish comfort in the sadness of those still on the dance floor—watching their former dance partners now dance with sorrow and anger and madness and grief. I came to realize that I would never be content with happiness found in sorrow. The validation of my meaning in life only occurred through the sadness of these lonely dancers that I once shared a dance with. This is not what I wanted.

Revitalized by the realization that I didn't want my previous dance partners sad all the time, I looked for new ways to contact my loved ones. It was still difficult—still frustrating. I was in a different plane of life since I left the dance floor. Communicating with the dancers was like mixing oil and water—very close, but never truly able to fully integrate.

As I toiled at my project of communication, I noticed the arrivals and departures of beings much like me. I had never really taken the time to look around my new environment since I had arrived here. I typically kept to myself except for an occasional visit with another frustrated soul. As I began to investigate further I realized that I had arrived at a place that was not truly independent of the rest of life. I had first assumed this place to be the final stop—it wasn't. It was a living world in motion. Not entirely different from the dance floor I was trying to contact.

I turned my attention to those souls departing this world. I asked where they were going—most didn't know, many had no idea at all. I asked why they were leaving. One looked at me as if I were a book he had already read. He said, "I came into this life; I thought about it; I did what I could for it; now I'm leaving it." I looked away momentarily stunned by my own words spoken so resolutely by this complete stranger.

I turned to speak more with the soul who read me so well. I wanted to hear more of what he had to say—the only words I heard him speak were so close to my own. The stranger had left. I asked those souls waiting to depart if they knew where he had gone. One soul turned to me and said, "He's gone. Are you his brother?" "No," I responded. "We had just met . . . Why?" The soul replied, "The stranger was about to leave when he looked at me and said, 'If you see my brother, tell him that I'm going to the dance.' He said his brother would know what he meant." I understood. I thanked the soul for the message and I danced away dreaming of all that could be.

I came to this new place from a dance; I thought about what to do when I got here; I will try to do it; and eventually I will probably leave. In the meantime, I will dance until it is time to go home to my family and friends. I hope you will do the same.

Lennon gave his mother & me the greatest gift the second he was born—his life. We had lost our previous child in a stillbirth, so when little Lennon came out bright-eyed and crying we were just happy/relieved beyond explanation. If you've ever had a stillborn child, that surreal experience becomes your expectation for any subsequent pregnancies. Lennon let us know loud and clear that that was the wrong expectation.

As for what I can say about Lennon now, he is probably the most like me of all my kids. He is the child that your own parents probably alluded to when you were growing up, when they said 'I hope someday you have children and they are exactly like you!'

That's basically what happened with Lennon. He's a great kid, but he is manipulative and delights in causing you to question why it is you are doing whatever it is you are doing. He's a wonderful little light who ultimately creates happiness while being more than willing to playfully challenge your knowledge on any topic.

How do you adequately parent a child who knows all your tricks? Be patient and let the other parent (if there is another parent) do all the heavy lifting? You are no match for a 4 year old who has read your playbook—they win every time.

Buck Jr, our 5th and youngest child, is 12 years younger than our oldest, Isaiah. We actually have two sets of kids 2 & 4 and then 12 & 14. We have many déjà vu moments in our house. The biggest difference among the lives of our children doesn't have so much to do with where they fall in birth order as it does with how old mom & dad were/are at varying points in their lives. I was 28 years old when Isaiah was born. I was 41 when Buck Jr was born. I think I mentioned that I used to be able to dunk a basketball (at 28 I probably still could), but at 41 I could barely touch the net, so the older set of kids got in-shape parents with stamina and whatnot and so forth; the second set of kids got parents who can't go from here to there without the snap, crackle, and pop of old bones along with the stamina you would expect from someone who snaps, crackles, and pops as they move.

Isaiah got way more attention from me than Buck Jr does for 2 reasons. First, I was younger and more energetic with Isaiah. Second, I only had one child with Isaiah, while I have had 5 with Buck Jr. So it really becomes a casualty of the law of diminishing returns as you have more children. You simply can't spend as much time with child #5 as you did with child #1. The hidden beauty of this situation is that the older children are full of energy and spend more time with the younger kids—not always, but much of the time.

So how can I be an adequate parent to Buck Jr (my youngest)? By being there when I can and letting the older children gain some parenting experience by tending to the younger kids. I wish I had endless amounts of time for all my kids, but that's a fool's dream that will never come true—so let the older kids take on some responsibility. Unless you're wealthy, you really don't have another choice and even if you are wealthy enough to hire a nanny, you'll be passing up an opportunity to help your kids grow both closer to each other and become more capable as parents in the future.

"Drugs are a difficult issue in our society," I stated. "Do you have any advice concerning the topic?"

"Absolutely," said Buck. "No matter how much of your personal experience you wish to divulge to your kids, somewhere within the conversation should be a warning: Drugs have the capacity to erase the past, distort the present, and end your future. I really don't have a problem with drug use in an abstract sense, but if you don't acknowledge the powers of addiction or are simply naïve to them, then I want you to know that the outlook is predictable and dim. You will wind up in a fight with a very powerful enemy that doesn't care, doesn't tire, and doesn't quit until you do—fair warning."

"Is that all on the subject of drugs?" I asked.

"Yes," responded Buck, "but as a more general suggestion regarding talking with your children, I suggest just doing your best. Talk to your kids at every age about whatever you're comfortable sharing & address their concerns as best you can. Like it or not your kids develop their thinking from you, as well as all sorts of non-verbal communication methods and mannerisms. You may be reluctant to talk very much for fear that they do, in fact, pick up your mannerisms, cognitive patterns and vocabulary. If this frightens you, just consider the alternative. Do you really want this task left to an uncaring world? Your kids will learn whatever it is they learn from somewhere and if it's not from you it will likely be from someone who simply doesn't care as much about them as you do. Perhaps that's sad commentary on the rest of the world, but the rest of the world leaves a bit to be desired."

"If you were to die immediately following this interview, what would you want me to say to the world on your behalf?" I asked.

"Nothing," responded Weedleman.

"Really?" I replied.

"I've said enough to the 'world'." Buck continued, "I would, however, have you convey a few thoughts to my family."

"What would you like to say to them?" I asked.

Buck stated, "I'd like to thank my parents. I aspire to reach their level of ability as a parent & I pray that the rest of the world's parents strive to achieve the same. Being an adequate parent is the most difficult job in the world. Being more than that requires divine intervention."

"To my kids: Please share each individual comment I just shared with you."

"To my wife: Thanks for taking this journey with me in good times and bad. Each day you become a more beautiful bride."

"Buck, I've noticed that you are not using much profanity during this interview," I observed. "Are you making a conscious effort not to swear?"

"Yes," he replied. "If you are familiar at all with any of my communication then you are well aware that I can rarely finish a sentence without some use of profanity. I don't use it for any other purpose than to make a point. You have probably noticed that I haven't used profanity even once during our conversation today—not yet anyway. I'm not sure this will land me in the good graces of my more dedicated followers really, but I'm already well into your questioning and have yet to use the 'f' word—there really is no substitute; had to break about 500 times to produce adequate substitute words and phrases for many of your more ubiquitous profanity. Sometimes profanity is simply the most concise way to communicate. I shouldn't have to search for alternative language because some prude somewhere might be offended."

"Why have you chosen not to use profanity during this interview?" I asked.

"Well," Weedleman started, "swearing allows people who hold different opinions than you do to automatically dismiss you and anything you have to say. This is sad, but a reality nonetheless."

Buck continued, "I find it interesting that most of the people who can dismiss an entire message simply because it contains profanity are the same folks that automatically dismiss other religions or races without knowing anything about the other religion/race. If I am so caught up in what I define as God that I can't even listen to someone else's conception or interpretation of 'God', should I really be taken seriously? Of course not. The defense of 'I'm right because I'm right' just isn't very persuasive. If you're so sold on how the universe works then welcome other views and defend your own. When I say to defend your religion, I mean to support it logically and peacefully. I am not promoting, or even condoning, making a violent stand. Religious folks talk a lot about peace, but seem to practice peaceful reconciliation very rarely."

"In any event," Buck went on, "I've abstained from the use of virtually all profanity during this interview, but don't get used to it. As I think about it, I can't help but be upset with myself to think that I would ever cave into peer pressure and not express ideas simply, in whatever manner I see fit. I don't censor others and their nonsense, so why is it acceptable for my ideas to be dismissed merely because of the method of delivery?"

After a pause for some eye rolling by a frustrated Weedleman, he continued. "Fine," Buck said with dismissive condescension, "if I use profanity you can dismiss my message without ever considering its substance based on its merits. We don't live in a meritocracy anyway so why should that be my expectation? Before you declare victory in this discussion of profanity, let's get back to the topic of much greater import—being an adequate parent."

"Very well," I said. "How does the use of profanity relate to parenting?"

"Profanity is just communication with a bit of an adrenalin rush," Weedleman stated. "It shouldn't automatically be assumed to be offensive. In fact, if your kids use profanity would you turn them away? If you dismiss what your child has to say because they use profanity then you are an abject failure as a parent. That may sound a little harsh, but the truth hurts sometimes. Actually if you reject your child because they use profanity they would probably do better on their own anyway. Ah *   *   * it, next topic."

"How do you feel about individual idiosyncrasies/proclivities/ habits/addictions? For example, how do you feel about smoking?" I asked.

"I'm against it," Buck was quick to respond. "It'll give you cancer. I wasn't going to mention this because it seems so dreadfully obvious. Many people smoke and that's fine I suppose for them, but in a day and age when nicotine can probably be delivered in the same fashion as caffeine—why insist on a delivery method that gives you cancer? I realize that we are a stubborn group—humans. But, are we really obstinate to the point of sacrificing our life to smoke? I really can't believe I have to discuss this, but in the interest of full disclosure I have to admit that I have smoked, but not when nicotine was readily available in other forms. I have absolutely nothing against nicotine. In fact, studies suggest that it reduces the risk of Alzheimer's and other cognitive disorders/diseases."

Buck continued, "So get out there and take in that nicotine, just do it without setting fire to your lungs. If you find that the only acceptable form of nicotine is via smoking then you need to make a long overdue appointment with a therapist—Dr. Freud had some interesting thoughts on smoking that you should investigate further."

"Is there a particular type of crime that angers you more than others?" I inquired.

"Domestic violence of any kind—directed toward any member of the family" replied Buck with a renewed sense of rage. "This is especially deplorable because it just goes on and on in plain sight. I have a solution for this. When the cops show up and they know who's guilty, but no one admits anything personally or makes a statement against the cowardly perpetrator, the solution is the Buck Weedleman Law. It's called the '2 visit 1 shot rule'. It goes like this; if the cops have to go to respond to a domestic violence call they first investigate—that's during the first call. If there is a subsequent second call to the same residence—they are required to shoot someone—no excuses—shoot the bad guy or woman (whoever). All these domestic violence situations have a victim and someone who needs to be shot—Buck's Law takes care of both. Of course that sounds harsh, but it fixes a problem that will otherwise not get fixed. Plus, while the police are now only making 2 calls to the residence instead of 5 million, they (the police) can be out catching criminals or preventing crime or writing tickets or eating doughnuts—whatever it is they do when they aren't wasting time on an endless parade of domestic dispute calls that usually end poorly for the victims and the perpetrator anyway.

"Do you have any thoughts regarding racism in our society today?" I asked expecting the typical politically correct answer that we've all come to despise. I was surprised.

Buck started, "To be an adequate parent with respect to other races requires honesty. For instance, have I ever used the 'n' word? Yes. I'm not running for office so I might as well be honest—the implication there is that to run for office requires dishonesty—probably true. Do I regret using the 'n' word? Yes. Before you condemn me, we really need to put this in the context of basic humanity. I have done many things that I regret—let those among you who don't have regrets cast the first stone."

Buck continued, "Have I been angered by someone to the point of abject virulence/violence—yep. I was going to go into this entire dissertation on the use of the 'n' word, why it's wrong and so forth, but I'm really not an expert on the subject. The simple truth is that I used that derogatory term that is offensive to virtually every reasonable person in a circumstance when my anger should have been focused on the person I had the problem with instead of on an entire race of people."

Buck stated defensively, "Please note that I apologized for using the term as it is degrading to a race of people who are undeserving of such degradation. I am not, however, apologizing to the specific person I referred to using the term that I now wish I hadn't. This is honesty. There exists on the face of this Earth white people that I do not like and there too exist black people that I do not like. I reserve the right to defend myself against those who would attack me. I apologize for a poor vocabulary that didn't allow proper focus on the individual, but rather generalized an entire race. What I meant to convey was the abject/utter/ complete/ sublime hatred that I had for specific individuals not entire races of people."

Weedleman continued, "People should not misdirect apologies. An apology must be sincere to have any meaning at all. I regret using the 'N' word—about that you can be certain, but I would be lying if I told you that I wished wonderful things for the person that I ignorantly referred to using the ugly term. I'm sure I disliked the person I referred to with the term. The only thing I can be certain of is that if I ever encounter the person again, I would use more appropriate ugly terms that focused solely on that person and not ignorantly on an entire race."

Buck went on, "If you're tempted to tell me to make peace with the people I truly don't like . . .—really just save that lecture for someone else. I don't like the people I don't like—it's just that simple & circular. Ironically enough given my 'n' word use admonition, I hate racists. I am an equal opportunity hater of many murderers with absolutely no regard for the color of their skin, but rather the content of their character. You'd have more luck convincing Israelis to embrace Hitler. Some see it as weakness not to forgive killers—I see it as justice to hunt them down—that's who I am."

"Let me give you an example of this sort of twisted political correctness," continued Buck. "In the 7th grade I remember a certain level of terrorism that was directed toward some innocent kids just standing in line for lunch at my middle school. In a moment of innocence you will understand the origin of virulence.

This violence wasn't a one time occurrence or even an occasional degradation, but rather an everyday torment. I remember that a group of 6 to 10 black kids would single out some white kid and 'ask' him for money. If the white kid didn't produce some money then the group of black kids would start using the 'n' word in a way that would implicate the white kid. For example, 'Did you just call me a n . . . ?' The cowards would typically continue the assault until the bell rang or a teacher would wander by or on a few occasions when another kid would intercede to try to protect the white kid getting bullied. The black kids just described weren't the 'n' word; they were cowards. They picked on a physically weaker kid. I was a relatively big kid back then—I never got picked on (picked on is a euphemism). I was never bullied or assaulted by this group of cowards. I'm a fight or flight type person. Looking back, I wish the group of useless cowards would have tried to bully me. I would have freaked out and killed them all. I'd probably still be in jail/prison for the 'hate' crime which ironically would be an appropriate description of the crime that I would have been charged with, despite it being self defense. I hated that group of 6 to 10 black kids not because they were black, but because they were garbage that terrorized innocent kids everyday. I'm not saying that there weren't white bullies—there were, but there was something particularly heinous and cowardly about the methods of the black bullies just described. They would throw out the 'n' word after which, of course, nobody would be allowed to even protect the victim because of what the perpetrators said the victim said. I'm not expecting fairness, but I, sure as hell, wish that I would have exacted a little justice, instead of standing paralyzed by a coward's use of 'the word that should not be uttered'. 'The word that should not be uttered' (but which can be referenced—in the proper context of course) = the 'n' word = J.K. Rowling's Voldemort = fear of the name only makes that name stronger = if we've learned nothing else from Harry Potter, and we haven't, it's that rendering a term off limits for any purpose only gives those wanting to cause harm with that word more power = c'mon people now, smile on your brother & stop fearing a word. I hate cowards. Hate's probably not a strong enough word. If you happen to be one of these cowards, recognize yourself as a disgrace to all that is good. You have no redemptive qualities. You do not belong to any race."

"There is a point at which truth must win out over cowardice and political correctness," stated Buck with conviction. "If you asked 100 random people if they ever used the 'n' word, about 50% of them might answer truthfully with 'No' while about 3% would answer truthfully 'Yes' which leaves 47% of the group lying—saying they hadn't used the 'n' word, but in fact have."

Weedleman continued, "The 'n' word is a term that implies that someone is less than human. It is offensive because of this meaning. It's a frightening word on a much deeper level because it was acceptable to use the term in America when referring to black people. Racism perpetuates itself because our society is slow to let go of traditional meanings no matter how wrong they are. There are still a measurable group of idiots out there that think the Earth is flat and that no one ever landed on the moon. These were traditional notions for a long time and various people just chose to continue to believe them—Why? Who knows really? Who cares maybe?"

"People may find this disappointing, coming from you, or even disturbing." I mused, "Are you worried about that?"

"I suppose," responded Weedleman, "but you wanted the truth right?"

"Yes," I said, "but this truth is difficult to accept while maintaining the same respect I had for you before I knew this truth."

"The truth is difficult," Buck replied. "People reject truth and fill the air with pleasant deception more often than they peacefully accept delivery of the truth. We should want to be delivered from evil to truth not giving in to the temptation to do what is easiest, to follow the path of least resistance, to live within the betrayal of political correctness. We should resist that temptation to be disingenuous. You will only find your genuine reflection in truth—To thine own self be true and that truth shall set you free—and so forth and whatnot."

"Aren't you worried about the visceral response you may evoke from telling this truth about yourself?" I asked.

"I fear no one (MLK)." Buck continued. "The blood I spill is done for you (JC). If you want blood, you got it (AC/DC). While I do not allow the use of the 'n' word in my house I also do not allow anyone to apologize for being white. Use of the 'n' word and the ridiculous notion that a white child should be born with a birth certificate and an accompanying certified apology for the color of their skin are truly among the most contemptible proclivities within society. I won't live in fear and I won't allow my children to be labeled inferior because of the color of their skin. I refuse to cater to the small minded. We should be judged not by the color of our skin, but rather the content of our character—I'm sure I've heard that before . . . (MLK)."

"You include yourself in pretty powerful company," I said wondering if he was equating himself with Dr. Martin Luther King, Jesus Christ, and Angus Young.

"Should I equate myself with weak company?" he responded rhetorically.

"If you want me to tell people simply what they want to hear, I'm afraid you're wasting your time. Besides, if you want pandering, just turn on your radio and listen for the amplified misguided voices of the institute for the advancement of personal gain through pandering," said Weedleman.

Buck was now either beginning to have fun or lose his sanity. In any event, he clearly showed no reservation. "I'm not one to typically just say that someone is an idiot and then not question why, but in this case I really don't know and I really don't care. Stated differently, I am contently ignorant and apathetic. The world is oval shaped. People landed on the moon. (and) No race of people is less than human. If you can't accept that, I've got nothing for you except that I think you're a hopeless irredeemable idiot. I like to think that no one is incapable of redemption, but I'm just not sure with this one. For now I think I'll just, as Sammy Hagar so aptly phrased it, "put it off until judgment day."

Buck continued, "Just about everything that I have ever written has been a thinly veiled attempt to give advice to my own children. I think I have a responsibility to give them a little dose of reality and help them to see how I actually deal or have dealt with that same reality. It really is too easy to just point to religion or culture or Oprah or Dr. Phil and say, 'just do whatever it is that they say to do. They will tell you what's right and wrong and will give you specific advice on how to live your life."

"Life is basically a movie in which we act and direct," said Weedleman. "There has never been a perfect movie—some are good, some are awful, some great, but most are mediocre, having good points and bad. Lives are like the books I've written. If I could write them again—would I? Probably, but at some point you have to say, 'enough with the editing—just get the book out there and available'. After all, I'm trying to give advice to the rising generation. I'm not giving a seminar on grammar or critical writing."

Buck became sentimental and admitted, "I've been pretty lucky in my life. I was born in a wonderful country, have wonderful parents, a wonderful wife, & wonderful kids. I have been lucky or blessed in my life, but my life is far from perfect—mostly because I and the world around me aren't perfect. Maybe you know someone perfect—I suppose we all need heroes & some of us need messiahs, but perfection's a tall order. I consider the pursuit of perfection as close to perfection as any of us will get."

Weedleman continued, "This is generally where all the advice I give to my kids winds up—just do what you see as necessary and important. Trying for anything more than that is just a painful exercise in the realization that we will never progress if we don't keep moving, even if it can only ever be in a less than perfect fashion/direction. In essence, we have a choice. We can lament the fact that the world and its inhabitants are imperfect or we can use what we know to better the world condition from where it is. Once you realize that you should celebrate the things that make the world better as much or more than you should hate the things that make the world evil at times, then you can truly live meaningfully. To simply lament the things that you can't change isn't living. The prayer, 'God grant me the serenity to accept the things I cannot change, the courage to change the things I can, & the wisdom to know the difference' is thoughtful and profound. If I could be granted one wish, it would be to know all the things that I could successfully make better. My Aunt Martha has this prayer posted on virtually everything she owns. She is a person of few words generally, but has said more to the world than I could ever hope to. She, by the way, was the first human to see me alive—as the attending nurse when I was born . . . cosmic/divine intervention?—Who knows, but the lesson of 'don't hate—celebrate'—(Warren Pearson—friend of mine's quote) continues and so does this interview—enjoy."

There was once a time," Buck continued, "That I thought that the world was so dreadfully lacking in goodness that the best we could collectively hope for as its citizens would be for some humanity erasing, apocalyptic event to simply end the madness once and for all. I was quite a fun person to be around then. Really—I was fun to be around. I saw no use in doing anything, but living for the moment. People like this are usually entertaining. They are reckless to the point of probably being dangerous to themselves and those around them, but certainly entertaining. I hope that I'm still entertaining—wouldn't be much hope for this interview if I opened with, 'I used to be entertaining, but not anymore—you should have known me then."

Buck took a reflective pause and said, "I see some hope for the world so I'm not quite so reckless anymore. However, I'm still very entertaining because the world is still very dangerous, unfair, & cruel. The best way that I have found to assimilate/accommodate the world into my brain is to laugh at the nonsense. Life is too important to take seriously—somebody else said that, but it bears repeating."

Buck's sanity really started to slip as he ventured into the world of business. "I have a favorite industry out there. I can't tell you the name of any specific businesses within that industry because I really have no need to benefit or defame anyone in that industry. So suffice it to say this is a fictional take on a real industry—like Oliver Stone's Wall Street, except not as good, but entertaining nonetheless. The industry I absolutely love creates awards. That's right. They create awards. They don't give awards for any specific act like the Oscar's or Emmy's. They don't just manufacture the little statues that are then embossed with the name of the deserving Nobel laureate or something like that. This industry will produce whatever award you want to give yourself. It markets this stuff primarily to salespeople who want to create the perception that they are successful and well respected within their industry and community. This is genius."

Buck continued his diatribe, "I don't have time to earn the respect of my peers, nor am I patient enough to waste half my life trying to find out if I'm truly good enough at something to get an award for it. The reality is that I think I'm great and since my opinion is the one I value most—Why not give myself an award? If you are an actor or musician or writer out there—why wait for your peers to acknowledge something that you are already well aware of? Give yourself that Oscar or Grammy or Pulitzer on behalf of your most important audience—you."

Buck continued on the topic of praising one's self, "I realize that everyone wants a little fame and money and the acknowledgement that they are meaningful, important, significant, & necessary, but has it really come to this? I happen to be self-indulgent and cheap so I just hand write whatever I feel people should know about me on notebook paper and tape it up in my office. People know right away that I gave myself an award, but with more expensive stuff people will probably figure it out eventually anyway so why not save a little money in the process. My award generally reads something like this: Buck Weedleman is truly the best communicator of stuff to other people—ever—in any medium—on any topic—in any forum—truly a beacon of hope—a glimmer of light in an otherwise dark world—a shining city on a hill (wait that was Reagan) & so on. Maybe I should try individual awards on 'Post-it' notes—more impact than one piece of notebook paper?" Buck continued. "I'll have to think about this one . . . perhaps a photo-shopped picture of me accepting the award from the Pope or the Dalai Lama or Jesus or somebody—give it a little more credibility/class. Maybe I could re-unite those 'We are the World' people from back in the 1980s and super-impose them on a nice plaque along with a recital of my accomplishments (or somebody's accomplishments anyway). I think I need this success-mill industry—I have finally sunk to new heights. Actually I think I've found a new business or at least a slogan to sell "Sink to new heights with Buck's Custom Awards Shop".

Buck had a few other notable business ideas (feel free to take them and run):

'Crucifixtures'—a line of plumbing supplies designed for the modern Christian home

'Jesus Saves—Now You Can Too—10% discount for qualified sinners'

'Ouch' brand medical supplies

'G/D Mosquitoes' brand bug repellant

'Shut the * * * up' brand bark collars for dogs

'Whose Child is it Anyway' brand home DNA kits

'So you think you can kick my * * *'—a guide for useful bar-room camaraderie

'Just dial the damn number'—a guide for the use of cell phones designed for Brokaw's 'Greatest Generation'

'Buck's Hospice—Just a Great Place to Die!'

'The Valley of the Shadow of Death and other Vacation Hot Spots'—a religious travel agency

Buck sat up and focused on us with a renewed motivation to instill more wisdom in us. He seemed to have found a moment of clarity—momentarily freed from his lapse in reason and perspective. "I must admit that I find Christmas movies redemptive, just, & happy. I'm not a huge fan of organized religion except to the extent that it is a system that creates peaceful places for people to gather. Benjamin Franklin belonged to many churches for just this reason."

Buck continued, "Maybe I am not that different from a religious person. A religious person wants an ultimate place that is redemptive, just, & happy (i.e. Heaven). So, just as I get lost in "It's a Wonderful Life", someone else may get lost in the Bible or the religious reference book of their choice—I don't know. I can tell you that few things are all good or all bad & religion is one of those ambivalent things. "It's a Wonderful Life" is all good except for the part where Uncle Billy puts the $8,000 in the g/d newspaper and gives the g/d paper to g/d old man Potter. My father in law told me that he could never watch that part of the movie. I find it difficult as well."

Weedleman continued with the Christmas theme, "I'm not a big fan of Christmas as a holiday really—too much commercialization, too much food, too much booze, too much everything except for quality time and patient tolerance. Conversations that begin with, 'How are you?' rarely end with the truth. Count the 'How are you?'s next Christmas. Maybe that should be the highlight of your next 'study'."

"May I make a dedication within this interview as I don't know what will become of me?" Weedleman inquired.

"Sure," I responded. "Is there something wrong?" I continued.

"No, but you never know . . . may I?" He again asked.

"Of course," I replied, "please go on."

"I would like to dedicate this interview and all of the enduring wisdom of Buck Weedleman to 100% of my immediate family, roughly 86-90% of my extended family, 16% of my friends, and to all the inhabitants of the island nation of Vito Alabamia—you are a proud, ignorant people destined to lose the battle of natural selection—bless your silliness and stupidity. I'll miss you loveable idiots once you've gone." Buck said very sincerely.

"In case you ever wondered, Buck, it's comments like that that make people believe that you are, in fact, crazy and not enlightened." I said.

"Huh," he replied, "that's unfortunate." He said dismissively then continued, "People think I'm crazy on this ship of fools—that hurts." He remarked sarcastically, rolling his eyes and shaking his head.

"Why do you have such outbursts?" I asked.

"Sometimes the craziness of the world just brings out the craziness in me. Isn't insanity the only sane reaction to an insane world? I love philosophy," he mused. "Let me give you an example; war and peace (not the novel, the concepts—war and peace). Give peace a chance. Wait about 6 minutes then send in the Marines."

I recalled hearing this from Buck on a separate occasion. It went something like this:

This is the sort of trite brilliance that Weedleman was capable of; this particular instance during a tailgate party at Miller Park in Milwaukee, WI. He was pretty drunk at the time and was later arrested for taking a whiz on a Milwaukee County police car. Buck's judgment was piss poor (once again not sure if the pun was intended) and while rarely lucid, he could occasionally hit a real homer (pun intended) as he did with this quote.

The quote was from later that same day at Miller Park when Buck inquired, "Don't you have better things to do?" A very profound statement really, in that we all could probably make the world a better place if we all just found something better to do. Sadly, the reality behind this brilliant utterance was that it was directed at the Milwaukee County cops who arrested Buck for whizzing on a squad car. The deeper meaning of this statement was lost on the officers. In fact, one officer was heard to say, 'Shut the * * * up you stupid-ass drunk', which is quite ironic now that we look back upon the savant-like wisdom of Weedleman. In further fact, Buck later alluded to this now infamous encounter within his truly inspired poem, "The Whizdom of Weedleman." While mostly known for his quick wit and busy liver/kidneys/bladder Buck had many ideas across many realms of society.

Buck was confident—recklessly so. This did not always serve him well as was the case with the Milwaukee police. He did benefit from his sense of self worth. I found this particularly intriguing. I wondered the source of his self esteem and how it could be instilled in the children of today. "How do you instill self confidence in a child?" I asked.

Buck said, "Let your child know that they are currently and will forever be extremely valuable while assuring them that they have the capacity to do many things that will challenge currently accepted limits within traditional notions of what is possible. Teach them to appreciate what and who they are while understanding the potential they possess to better the universe around them."

"Is that the same advice you have for adopted children, children with disabilities, or children of mixed races or blended families?" I continued.

Buck shot back angrily, eyes obviously searing red, "If you draw a distinction among adopted kids, kids with disabilities, kids from blended or mixed families, red, white, yellow or brown kids, and any other kids then you CANNOT be an adequate parent. You're just too stupid. Such ignorance just takes me back to the fact that the world needs to require people to pass a test BEFORE they can be allowed to procreate! To answer your ridiculous question: of course I would give the same advice to all children. A kid is a kid!"

Buck continued, "I attended a lecture on diversity at a place that I worked—all employees, required attendance, you know the drill. I found the speaker quite interesting in that he refused to accept the idea of multiple races. He suggested that the implication of multiple races connotes the ceaseless assumption that one or the other race is inferior to another. Since all races, in this context, are human, to think of one as inferior suggests that some races are human and some are sub-human. He believed that we are all subjected to, or products of, varying cultures, but not fundamentally different. I have to agree."

"You're advice may make me the best parent ever." I said thinking myself clever.

Weedleman let me have it, "So you're going to be the BEST parent EVER, aye? No you're not. You know who I was going to be when I grew up? Preston Pearson; Preston Pearson grew up in my home town and later played for the Dallas Cowboys. You know who else I was going to be when I grew up? Eddie Van Halen. Don't you remember anything I just said? Check your notes! You can commit whatever energy and resources you have to becoming someone or something, but it may never happen. What can happen is that you can become an adequate football player or guitarist if you simply lower the bar a little. You have to learn to walk before you can run—I don't know if that's true either. Maybe some babies just take off running—who knows? The larger point here is that you can be good enough at many things. With respect to parenting you really owe it to your child(ren) to become an adequate parent. Start there. Just being adequate at parenting takes more work than most people are willing to take on. However, it's important for everyone to remember that you can't give up being a parent like I gave up football and my quest to be a rock star."

"So get ready America," Buck shot out. "I am going to crush what you think you know about being great and replace it with the lowered expectations that will allow you to be pretty good or, at least, not bad."

"How?" I asked.

"I can give you practical advice that is useful in realistic situations, not lofty unattainable goals," said Buck and then continued, "Let's start with soccer."

"Soccer?" I repeated with a puzzled look on my face. Here's Buck's take on soccer:

"Soccer is as good a place as any to start being an adequate parent." Weedleman said in a determined voice, "I won't rest until all of you go to your kids' soccer games—just go, don't coach! Since most of you don't know the first thing about soccer anyway, just sit there in your lawn chair and clap when the people around you do. That's why parents of kids on the same team sit together, so that collectively they can figure out when to clap. If you find some kid from another country, get your kid on his or her team. The rest of the world understands soccer. Just mill around that kids parents and clap when they do. Write down a few things they yell onto the field. Then, make some flashcards with these various sayings/ yellings and yell them out from time to time at the next game. The order in which you yell them out doesn't matter. No one will know if you are making sense or not, except the couple from who knows where, and they're probably so sick of explaining soccer to Americans that they won't even call you out on your mistakes. I spend most of my soccer games sitting on a lawn chair reading a paper on the sidelines of a soccer field with a bunch of 7 or 8 year olds playing on the field, my parents on either side talking (at) to me, and my wife in the background talking to some other parent while no one is really paying attention to the game. The realistic significance of this is that an adequate parent gets his/ her child to the game and supports their efforts and interests with their attendance. Expecting a whole lot more, however, is often so unrealistic that it is a recipe for failure."

"You've spoken about your family before. Anything you'd like to add?" I asked.

Buck responded, "My own experience with my father has gone something like this; At first I thought that he was invincible—that lasted until my mid-teens or so (then) I saw him as a bit naïve and needing my protection. I remember one incident in particular when my dad came to visit me at college. We had gone into the college town to get some groceries for me. While we were leaving my dad drove out of the parking lot uncertain of which exit we should use to go where-ever we were going next. In driving with this sort of uncertainty another driver yelled, "Stupid" in a sort of dumb sounding voice. Now I am not the size of Hulk Hogan nor do I fight like an MMA (Mixed Martial Arts) fighter, but at that time I was about 19 or 20 years old, playing football and swimming in college. I was in the best shape of my life & some idiot just called my dad stupid. I saw red. That's all I saw. I wanted blood, the only currency I would accept from the other driver. My hypothalamus, the part of the brain that regulates aggression, just gave the order for all out war. For fans of Adam Sandler's The Waterboy he activated my medulla oblongata." Buck continued to speak of his father. "My dad has always been pretty smart; and far more reserved than I am—as the guy from my college years example almost found out. Part of me still wishes I would have caught that guy even though I'd still probably be in a Wisconsin prison somewhere. But who knows, it may have been worth it. I guess I'll never know."

Buck continued, "I think that had it not been for my mom being with us, I would have jumped out of my parent's car, pulled that guy out of his and beat him to death. I wish I were exaggerating, but I'm not. I suppose I could be exaggerating, since you never really know what you actually would do in any given situation until you actually go through that situation. Maybe I wouldn't have beaten that rude stranger to death, if my mother hadn't been present, but I tend to believe that I would have—even to this day some 25 years later."

"Do you have any others advice to offer parents?" I asked.

"Sure," he responded. "If you set your standards too high in parenting you wind up being awful at it. Well not all of us, but most. Most of the time I'm an adequate parent, but there are periodic lapses. I've given such parental advice as, 'Well, you're going to have to get even with him.' and 'You just can't lie all the time. It isn't practical.'"

Buck went on, "I am much like my own parents as they were always perfecting, not perfect, always trying to teach, even now as I'm in my 40s and my dad is in his 70s. For example, I saw my dad this weekend and he gave me the game section of the newspaper and said 'do this', so I did. Honestly, I did about 30% of it, got stumped, gave up, and gave it back to my dad. He filled in one of the answers and gave me back the paper saying, 'You should be able to get more of them now'. So, I did some more and gave it back to him. This process continued until "I" had completed the crossword puzzle & every other game in that section of the paper. Anyway, my dad continues to teach me to keep my mind active with his persistence. I don't think a parent ever stops trying to teach their kids. I know my dad hasn't."

Maybe that's why," he said reflectively, "I keep granting interviews and writing as I have . . . because it keeps the energy coursing through my brain. Of course my parents have read my writing, and my dad still encourages crosswords. I think my parents, my dad specifically, is telling me what he has told his students (he taught math almost his whole life)—you are capable of far more than you generally think you are—so get out there and be amazed at what you can do."

Buck then said a few things about his mom, "My mom is easy to describe, yet difficult to understand—like most people I suppose. She loves me and my brother and our wives & the grandchildren & my dad. She has in common with my wife, mother-in-law and my grandmothers the need to let me know that she loves me. That sounds simple, but it's profound. I have used this quote from Maya Angelou in a book I wrote, but it's worthy of repeating, "There is nothing more eloquent than a parent saying, 'I love you' to a child." Bill Clinton said that all a child needs to excel in life is to know that he or she is important to one person. If you let someone know that they are important to you, that is, perhaps, the most positive and powerful influence you will ever have on their life. At a very basic level, I know that I'm important because my mom thinks that I am. That's powerful stuff. Perhaps the hand that rocks the cradle truly is the hand that rules the world—'And the Cradle Will Rock'. Not to further obsess on the guy that called my dad stupid, that I was subsequently going to beat to death, but had he called my mother something less than flattering, I'd still be looking for him today (or I would have found him and the search for him would be left to police cadaver dogs—zombie hunters). The mother-child relationship is strong and you tamper/trifle with it at your own risk."

We are almost out of time," I said. "Is there any parting thoughts you would like to share?"

"Sure," Weedleman responded. "Let your kids know you, even if that means letting them know you, then listen to them, answering their questions as honestly as you can."

Buck went on, "I hate to paraphrase Dr. Phil or Oprah in here, but one of them said that it's important to talk about the little things so that you have practiced a method of talking about the big things—they're correct. Look, if you can't even talk about baseball or the weather with your kids it will be virtually impossible to talk to them about bigger events like drugs, death, gangs, God, guns, race, rights, religion, and of course the music of Eddie Van Halen. I use EVH as an example a lot. As I mentioned before this is really just an effort to get him to comment on the interview, thus increasing sales and therefore making me more money—very selfish I know, but I don't care—so we may as well continue with the example. EVH toured with his 16 year old son, Wolfgang Van Halen. My wife and I along with my 2 oldest kids who were 12 & 10 at the time saw them in Chicago and Milwaukee—great shows."

Buck continued to discuss EVH, "In any event, I think that EVH can teach us all an important parenting lesson—be as honest as you can with your kid(s) & talk to them about the little things—like being a rock star if that's what you happen to know. EVH has had addiction problems, but has never really lied to anyone about this reality. Suppose he had successfully lied to his son and the world about his addictive personality—then WVH grows up with those same addictive proclivities and thinks that they should be a source of secret shame? How do most people deal with secret shame? They distort it with some inebriant—they get high or drunk or do something that warps their reality. We could all learn a lot from EVH and that ain't just rock 'n roll . . ."

Buck continued relating his thoughts on parenting within the confines of his own family, "In any event, I became protective of my dad from about my late teens until I had kids of my own. In the last 14 years I have seen my kids look to me as invincible. I have also seen them look to me as naïve and in need of protection. We are all powerful & naïve to a certain extent. We don't like to admit the naïve part, but such are the limitations of the human condition. I realize that this sounds like a tribute to my own parents more than a 'how to' for the purposes of being an adequate parent. Suffice it to say that if you think that you have the opportunity to teach your child something—do it & if you feel like telling your child that they are important to you (that you love them) then do that too. You'll at least be an adequate parent if you do these things—probably even break into the exceptional parent rankings."

Bucked continued a little exhausted from a taxing discussion. "At this point you need to know one of the basic realities of human beings common to all—the earlier in your life we understand something the more impact it has. For example, if it takes me until my kids are 47 years old before they understand that I think that they are important it will take a lot more convincing than if I would have told them that same thing when they were 7 or 3 years old or an infant or even in the womb (who really knows what goes on in there). Plus, you never know if you will make it to see them turn 47 or even sadder they may not make it to 47. Let them know they are important—today—now. Really—call them now genius—you'll feel better and so will they."

Buck continued, "One more note on this. If you have lost a child, (1) I am sorry, (2) I can't change what happened, (3) I don't really know what happens to people when they die, (4) I have lost a child, (5) you should talk to them in meditation or prayer or some other way & tell them they are important, (6) I don't know if #5 actually works, (7) #5 might actually work so do it—today—now, (8) now (and), (9) your child wants you to be at peace just as you want them to be at peace."

My next topic for Buck to address was that of sex, particularly how a mere mortal should explain such an easily misunderstood, yet important aspect of human existence to their children. "What is your advice to parents regarding explaining sex to their children?" I asked.

"Talk to your kids about it, so they at least don't make the same mistakes that you did or miss the opportunities that you did (same coin—different sides)," was his simple response.

"Buck, you spoke about the dangers of drug use earlier. Do you have anything further to add to your advice as it relates to discussing drug use with your children?" was my next question.

"Talk to your kids about it," Weedleman replied, "so they at least don't make the same mistakes that you did. The real danger with drugs is dancing with hypocrisy. You've done whatever you've done in your life and you can choose to share that with your kids or not, but tell them if there are things in your past that you won't be talking about if that, in fact, is the case. Lying is easy to do, but difficult to be good at. Your kids will probably know that you smoked pot, if you smoked pot, but they won't know you're a liar until you tell them that you didn't smoke pot if, in fact, you did.

I'm as honest as I can be with my kids; which is to say that I'm about as honest with them as I am with myself. In practice this means that I didn't tell them much about things that I have little recollection of myself or things that I truly regret. The things that we truly regret probably aren't adequately processed by our own brains—so leave those topics to a therapist. Tell your kids that life without regrets is a riskless waste of time, but that pushing too far in any direction is dangerous. To recap, yes—tell your kids that you have done things that upon further reflection you wish you hadn't, but don't throw specifics out there unless you are ready to give some meaning to those specifics. Odds are that you don't know why you drank too much, ate too much, smoked too much, etc. I suggest letting them know you're not perfect and moving on. After all, that is a life lesson they will surely need—knowing when to just move on. If you dwell too much on mistakes you will never know success," explained Buck.

"I s money important and what role should it play in our society?" I inquired.

"Within the arsenal of useless things that I tend to repeat includes these gems." Buck started with a series of quotes.

"If you want to know what God thinks of money, just look at who he gives it to."—Dorothy Parker

"Being Rich is better than being poor if only for financial reasons."—Woody Allen

"Money may not buy you love, but honestly that wasn't going to be my first purchase."—Comedian on the Bob & Tom radio program

Weedleman went on, "This is all true enough, but most of us won't have a lot of money during our lives, so don't spend your life obsessing on it. You have about as much control over how much money you have as you have control over the weather. So like with the weather, learn about it and respect its power, but don't let that worry consume and compromise the quality of your life. There is an amount of money/security that we all need in order to survive, but beyond that amount of necessary fundage, money is more a diversion of progress and creativity than an instigator of it. The question, 'How can I get rich?' usually results in the type of nonsense you can watch on an infomercial. Besides, 99% of the wealth in the world is inherited, not earned; ergo, 99% of the wealthy are frauds on themselves and society."

Buck continued, "I talk with some people regarding money & they will invariably bring up Bill Gates or Thomas Edison or Warren Buffet and then try to connect the dots between success and wealth. There is a causation problem with the argument that Bill Gates developed computer science to get rich. Yes, Bill Gates became rich because of his development of computer science and general business acumen, but had he not found a profitable application for the computer, he would still be a nerd talking up the possibilities inherent with gigabytes or tachyons or whatever occupies his brain. Would Elvis have stopped singing if it wouldn't have been profitable? Of course not. The 'profit motive' results in infomercial garbage. True riches in society are intrinsically motivated by the need to build or understand or cure—to be significant in some way."

Buck was on his soap box, yet strangely calm and convinced of his correctness, "If you really want to solve all global economic issues/problems you would mandate that virtually all the money in an estate escheat back to the state after the death of someone. Exempt $10 million or so for the good-for-nothing heirs of the decedent, but take the rest—take all the rest. First, we as society shouldn't be ruled by a hand from the grave—the decedent. Second, if the money makers were truly driven by the 'profit motive' then that genetically passed pre-disposition will be lost if the money is already there by way of inheritance. If you really want to see innovation then make Bill Gates poor again and watch him claw/innovate his way back. Give him and his heirs reason to innovate—make them poor."

Buck went on, "Don't teach your kids to chase money. Money isn't necessarily a bad thing, but to the extent it diverts attention away from more meaningful pursuits, it truly is 'as wicked as it seems'—Keith Richards," Weedleman replied then continued, "Wealth is what remains when you successfully learn to turn a blind eye to those in need. Success is never turning a blind eye to those in need. Success and wealth, therefore, are mutually exclusive."

"I know your time with us is just about up. Is there anything that you would like to tell us (on any variety of topics)?" I asked.

"Sure," he replied. "But I must warn you that I don't remember what I should remember, let alone communicate to others what I should or shouldn't for that matter. I guess that makes me the perfect confidant—forgetful and empathetic. You will forever live in the memory of your first experiences because it is at those points that cognitive tracks are established in your brain/mind/spirit. Why do you remember your first love in a different category than the rest? Because your mind was a blank slate to be written on & no matter how you try to erase that first experience a faded image of it will always exist. As life goes on you will overwrite what appears on the "slate" of your mind with bolder, more substantial color, texture, & intensity—more meaning. Optimists think about the possibilities of tomorrow, while pessimists dwell/ruminate on the mistakes of yesterday. Just as I don't trust the world around me, I don't expect you to trust the world around you—including me. No one truly knows what they are capable of—good or bad. I routinely attend The Church of Wishful Thinking led by the Reverend Billy Joe Armstrong as well as Holy Christ Almighty by way of the Onion Order of Theologians. With respect to peer pressure—know when to blend in & when to stand out. Caveat accompanying all those listening: while the past may not be the best predictor of the future, it's really all we have to work with. Work is necessary, but mislabeled. Most of us see work as a sort of punishment or payment for being alive. I know that I have thought of it in those terms, plus I'd be lying if I said I don't routinely look forward to the weekends, but work doesn't have to be a punishment. The key is to try and find something that interests you. Tuesday is always going to be Monday's hangover."

"You have an opinion on virtually everything," I said. "Can you give me an opinion on Jesus?"

With sanity once again in short supply Buck responded with this, "Jesus owes me money, but I'm willing to forgive. Honestly—20 dollars. Now I'm not saying that I've never welshed on a bet, but he's Christ for chrissake. It should really work like this:

Things To Do for JC

1. Do unto others . . .

2. Feed the hungry

3. Pay Buck his g/d 20 bucks

You may be wondering what we were betting on. I bet $20 that he couldn't turn water into wine—we've all heard the stories . . . Long story short, he turned some of the murkiest sludge known to any eco-system into the most righteous malted beverage ever to splash out of the Pecatonica River. Why did I win? The bet was about wine. Once you barley up some hops in some sort of malting process, you've made beer my friend—not wine. So I'm explaining all this and he's laughing it off. But I'm serious. I needed the money and Jesus or not, he made beer not wine & it was time to break out the Holy wallet and pay up. It's been several years now & I doubt I'll ever see the cash. It's the principle really—like he couldn't skim the plate a little on Sunday for 20 bucks. Christ, this still pisses me off."

Buck started to conclude, "In my other interviews I quoted far more lyrics from far more musicians. But with this one I just can't get no satisfaction. I got 57 channels and nothin' on. I did speak about my children of the sun, but generally all I find is darkness on the edge of town. However, no dark sarcasm in the classroom can adequately portray the blue days and black nights that leave us all thunderstruck. I spoke briefly about suspicious minds and the paranoid, but you really just need to free your mind, don't be cruel, and if all else fails, somebody get me a doctor 'cause it's cool when you cause a cozy condition, but you say you want a revolution? You got another thing comin'—an eruption on the dark side of the moon. I want to be sedated on this crazy train. Hey you, breakin' the law, livin' after midnight, get off of my cloud. It doesn't matter if you're black or white cause you're on the road to nowhere. How about a little sympathy for the devil? The time has come for you my friend to all this ugliness we must put an end. This is the end, my only friend the end & in the end the love you take is equal to the love you make."

Buck was now clearly exhausted, walking erratically between sanity and psychosis, "My life started like most of yours. I found myself in a world not knowing the origin of my being. I called what I sensed around me 'reality'. From my reality I moved around by choice and necessity. With my travels came understanding & understanding demanded further travel; travel through the reality that availed itself to me. Reality is what is left when optimism and pessimism are at equilibrium. Your questions are fit for a fool so I am completely comfortable answering them. Life is a balance of sanity, survival, and the sublime."

Buck began to withdraw back into the comfort of his contrived, delusional reality. I let him go. He had given us enough. As with many of us, he is a good person at a very basic level. I had no reason to push Buck Weedleman or any other good person beyond what they can contend with. I would never push anyone beyond their capabilities—that would be cruel; lacking in compassion for the individual while serving no constructive or meaningful purpose. I simply said 'Thank you' at this point. Buck responded by saying something about the residual value of one red sock. I think that I may have pushed him a little too far. He was clearly now absent from our conversation. He excused himself from our table, meandered a bit then wandered out the door. As he left I wasn't sure whether I should call him a cab or try and get him to a psych ward, detox perhaps. As for myself I was mentally and emotionally exhausted by this time; in many ways Buck had sacrificed his sanity for mine by challenging me to join in the contemplation of our collective existence. That was the last we saw of him.

The sad reality of a true genius is probably loneliness. It's ironic that Buck is always in great demand and yet still very alone even within the constant attention. Buck is like a marathon runner that never loses a race; he is always alone in front of the pack unable to relate to the other runners because he never has anyone to chase. He has no model to follow to get faster. He must blaze his own trail, occasionally slowing down to inspire other runners to pass him so that he can rest in the wake of another's thoughts/understanding/knowledge/wisdom. Lonely for sure—a sad existence mixed with unmatched perspective. Keep running, Buck. We will catch up someday.

Over the course of this interview I'm certain that you've grown in the wisdom of Buck Weedleman. While some see Buck as merely an endless wellspring of self-promotion and nonsense, others like you and I are better than that. We accept Buck into our lives as the semi-fictitious, omnipotent, omnipresent, omniscient being that is both simultaneously merciful and angry. We fear and love him because at the end of the day we don't know much about anything so we take comfort in believing that Buck is out there watching over our every move with an absolute grip on right, wrong, good, evil, etc.; availing those powers to enforce the aforementioned concepts/constructs in a pure and just manner.

I hope you enjoy your religion as much as I do mine. Amen.